Anonymo

The Publications of the Harleain Society
Society
Volume III

Salzwasser

Anonymous

The Publications of the Harleain Society
Volume III

1. Auflage | ISBN: 978-3-84605-058-3

Erscheinungsort: Frankfurt, Deutschland

Erscheinungsjahr: 2020

Salzwasser Verlag GmbH

Reprint of the original, first published in 1870.

THE

PUBLICATIONS

OF

The Harleian Society.

ESTABLISHED A.D. MDCCCLXIX.

Volume III.

FOR THE YEAR MDCCCLXX.

TAYLOR AND CO., PRINTERS,
LITTLE QUEEN STREET, LINCOLN'S INN FIELDS.

The Visitation of the County of

Rutland

In the Year

1618-19.

TAKEN BY

WILLIAM CAMDEN

Clarenceux King of Arms.

AND OTHER DESCENTS OF FAMILIES NOT IN THE VISITATION.

EDITED BY

GEORGE JOHN ARMYTAGE, F.S.A.,

HONORARY SECRETARY TO THE SOCIETY.

LONDON:

1870.

At a Meeting of the Council of the HARLEIAN SOCIETY, *held at 8, Danes Inn, London, W.C., on the 22nd day of June, 1870, the* HON. HENRY ROPER-CURZON *in the Chair, it was resolved that—*

" The VISITATION OF RUTLAND IN 1618, *to be edited by the Honorary Secretary, be the Second Publication for the Present Year."*

Preface.

Of the small county of Rutland there are but two Visitations, viz. one made in the year 1618, and the other in 1681–2.

The original of the first of these is in the College of Arms (marked C. 14), where there is also a copy with additions by Vincent. There are also copies in the British Museum, as mentioned below. The other Visitation (viz. that of 1681–2) is in the College of Arms (marked K. 1.). Of this, it is believed, there is no other copy out of that College.

The following volume contains the Visitation of 1618, with additions, and is compiled from the manuscripts in the British Museum that relate to that Visitation. The general text is taken from Harl. MS. 1558. The arms in that MS. are tricked by Richard Munday, and the descents are considerably extended beyond the period of the Visitation. The order of the pedigrees is taken from the Harl. MS. 1094, which is the same order as that in the College of Arms. The descents after page 26 are, however, not contained in this last-named MS., but are entirely supplied from the MS. 1558, and are probably copied from the additions made by Vincent in his own MS., now preserved in the College of Arms, as mentioned above.

The Visitation of Rutland in the Harl. MS. 1094 is written and the arms tricked by John Withie, and commences at page 230 of that MS.

For the convenience of the members of this Society, a list of the pedigrees in the Visitation of 1681 is here appended.

Barker of Hambleton and Lindon.

Beacham of Branston and Seaton.

Brown of Stockenhall and Clipsham.

Brown of Tolethorp and Uppingham.

Burton of Okeham and Eyton.

Busby of Barlithorp.

Fawkener of Stoke Dry, Braunston, and Uppingham.

Halford of Edith Weston.

Hippisley of Hambleton.

Horsman of Stretton.

Huggeford of Glaston.

Hunt of Barradon.

Johnson of South Luffenham and Clipsham.

Mackworth of Normanton.

Mathew of Okeham.

Noel of Brook and Whitwell.

Noel of Exton and South Luffenham (Viscount Campden, Lord Noel, etc.).

Pelsant (afterwards Buswell of Lidington).

Sherard of Whitsundine.

Wright of Okeham.

There are many references in the MSS. from which this volume has been taken to the Visitation of Leicestershire : these have all been carefully transcribed, and the number of the pages of that Visitation as printed in the second volume of the Society's publications has been inserted in brackets.

The Index has been compiled by Mr. F. R. Armytage, of Balliol College, Oxford, a member of the Society.

GEO. J. ARMYTAGE,

Hon. Sec.

List of Pedigrees.

The Visitation of the County of Rutland,

COMMENCED IN THE YEAR 1618, AND CONTINUED IN THE YEAR 1619; TAKEN BY AUGUSTINE VINCENT, ROUGE ROSE PURSUIVANT OF ARMS, MARSHALL AND DEPUTY UNTO WILLIAM CAMDEN, CLARENCEUX. (HARL. MSS. 1094 AND 1558.)

(Harbottell.)

ARMS. *Quarterly of six:*—1. *Azure, three icicles bendways or.* HARBOTTEL. 2. *Argent, three escallops gules.* WELWICK. 3. *Argent, three water-pots covered gules.* MOUNBOUCHER. 4. *Per pale azure and gules, three chevrons charged with as many couped and counterchanged.* SAY. 5. *Gules, five fusils conjoined in fess, each charged with an escallop sable.* CHENEY. 6. *Or, a chief gules, over all on a bend engrailed azure an annulet of the field.* HARRINGTON.
CREST. *A dexter arm embowed vested azure, the cuff argent, holding in the hand proper a club or.*

Roger Harbottell Lord of Harbottell. Temp. H. 1.=

Bryan Harbottell Esq[r].=. . . d. & heire of S[r] Roger Welwick.
ARMS. *Argent, three escallops gules.*

Thomas Harbottell Esq.=Mary d. of S[r] John Fenwick Knight.

. . . d. of S[r] John Witherington Knight. 1 wife.=S[r] John Harbottell Knight.=. . . d. of S[r] John Lowther of . . . Knight 2 wife.

Humfrey Harbottle sonn of S[r] John.=Isabell d. of John Millott.
ARMS. *(Argent), on a bend cotised (gules) three billets (sable).*

S[r] Widyard Harbottle of Com' Northumbland Knight.=Diana da. of Sir Will'm Hilton Knt.
A. 2 Bars B.

A

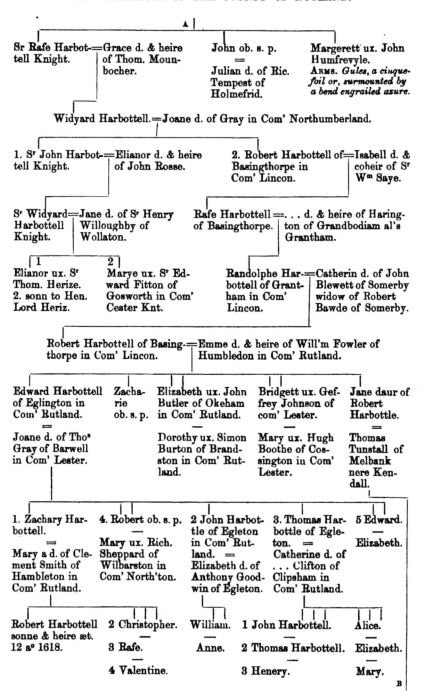

Sr Rafe Harbot-=Grace d. & heire
tell Knight.   of Thom. Moun-
                bocher.

John ob. s. p.
=
Julian d. of Ric.
Tempest of
Holmefrid.

Margerett ux. John
Humfrevyle.
ARMS. *Gules, a cinque-
foil or, surmounted by
a bend engrailed azure.*

Widyard Harbottell.=Joane d. of Gray in Com' Northumberland.

1. Sr John Harbot-=Elianor d. & heire
tell Knight.   of John Rosse.

2. Robert Harbottell of=Isabell d. &
Basingthorpe in   coheir of Sr
Com' Lincon.   Wm Saye.

Sr Widyard=Jane d. of Sr Henry
Harbottell Willoughby of
Knight.   Wollaton.

Rafe Harbottell =. . . d. & heire of Haring-
of Basingthorpe. ton of Grandbodiam al's
                  Grantham.

1   2
Elianor ux. Sr   Marye ux. Sr Ed-
Thom. Herize.   ward Fitton of
2. sonn to Hen.   Gosworth in Com'
Lord Heriz.   Cester Knt.

Randolphe Har-=Catherin d. of John
bottell of Grant- Blewett of Somerby
ham in Com'   widow of Robert
Lincon.   Bawde of Somerby.

Robert Harbottell of Basing-=Emme d. & heire of Will'm Fowler of
thorpe in Com' Lincon.   Humbledon in Com' Rutland.

Edward Harbottell
of Eglington in
Com' Rutland.
=
Joane d. of Thos
Gray of Barwell
in Com' Lester.

Zacha-
rie
ob. s. p.

Elizabeth ux. John
Butler of Okeham
in Com' Rutland.
=
Dorothy ux. Simon
Burton of Brand-
ston in Com' Rut-
land.

Bridgett ux. Gef-
frey Johnson of
com' Lester.
=
Mary ux. Hugh
Boothe of Cos-
sington in Com'
Lester.

Jane daur of
Robert
Harbottle.
=
Thomas
Tunstall of
Melbank
nere Ken-
dall.

1. Zachary Har-
bottell.
=
Mary a d. of Cle-
ment Smith of
Hambleton in
Com' Rutland.

4. Robert ob. s. p.
—
Mary ux. Rich.
Sheppard of
Wilbarston in
Com' North'ton.

2 John Harbot-
tle of Egleton
in Com' Rut-
land. =
Elizabeth d. of
Anthony Good-
win of Egleton.

3. Thomas Har-
bottle of Egle-
ton. =
Catherine d. of
. . . Clifton of
Clipsham in
Com' Rutland.

5 Edward.
—
Elizabeth.

Robert Harbottell
sonne & heire æt.
12 aº 1618.

2 Christopher.
—
3 Rafe.
—
4 Valentine.

William.
—
Anne.

1 John Harbottell.
—
2 Thomas Harbottell.
—
3 Henery.

Alice.
—
Elizabeth.
—
Mary.

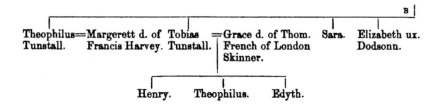

B |

Theophilus=Margerett d. of Tobias   =Grace d. of Thom.   Sara.   Elizabeth ux.
Tunstall.   Francis Harvey. Tunstall. | French of London   Dodsonn.
                                       Skinner.

Henry.   Theophilus.   Edyth.

"Thus sett out in the vissitation in the office." 1. *Harbottell.* 2. *Wellwick.*
3. *Mounboucher.* 4. *Harington.*

Corbett.

ARMS. *Or, three ravens sable, in chief a martlet gules for difference.*

Corbett of Ponsbery in Com' Sallop.

1. John   3. Arthur Corbett of Wanlyp=Mary d. of Hugh Bradshaw of   2. Edward
Corbett.   in Com' Lester.   Moorebarne in Com' Lester.   Corbett.

2. Thomas   3. Roger Corbett=Mary d. of Thom.   4. Humfrey Corbett of London
Corbett   of Hatherne in | Clarke of . . . in   marchantalor m. Agnes d. of
ob. s. p.   Com' Lester.   Com' Lester.   Geo. Jue of Haddam in Com'
                                                  Hertford & ob. s. p.

1 Arthur   2 Humfrey   Anne d. of Sir Edward=3. Roger Corbett of Stoke New-
Corbett   Corbett   Fowler of Islington | ington in Com' Midlesex slaine
ob. s. p. ob. s. p.   in Com' Midlesex   by mishap in a pond 5 of Oc-
                       Knt.   tober 1639.

Edmond.   Mary.   Ann.   Sarah.

1. Christopher Corbett of Wanlyp in Com'=Anne* d. of John Wymarke of
Leicester & of Stretton in Com' Rutland. | North Luffenham in Com' Rutland.

Elinor ux. Peter Mandes   Wiburga ux. Edward   Elizabeth ux. .... Owen
of Denton in Com' Lincon.   Smythe of Norcott in   of Lester towne.
                               Com' Rutland.

A |

* Dorothy in Harl. MS. 1094. See also Visit. Leicester, p. 48.

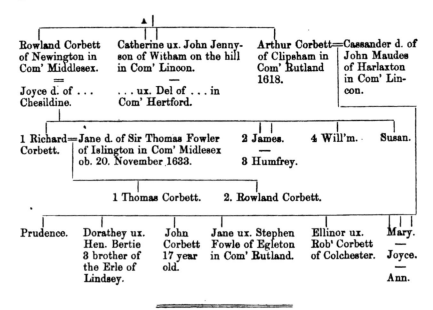

Rowland Corbett
of Newington in
Com' Middlesex.
=
Joyce d. of ...
Chesildine.

Catherine ux. John Jenny-
son of Witham on the hill
in Com' Lincon.
—
... ux. Del of ... in
Com' Hertford.

Arthur Corbett=Cassander d. of
of Clipsham in | John Maudes
Com' Rutland | of Harlaxton
1618. | in Com' Lin-
| con.

1 Richard=Jane d. of Sir Thomas Fowler   2 James.   4 Will'm.   Susan.
Corbett. | of Islington in Com' Midlesex   —
| ob. 20. November 1633.   3 Humfrey.

1 Thomas Corbett.   2. Rowland Corbett.

Prudence.   Dorathey ux.   John   Jane ux. Stephen   Ellinor ux.   Mary.
| Hen. Bertie   Corbett   Fowle of Egleton   Rob' Corbett   —
| 3 brother of   17 year   in Com' Rutland.   of Colchester.   Joyce.
| the Erle of   old.   —
| Lindsey.   Ann.

(Butler.)

ARMS. *Quarterly of six:*—1. *Gules, a fess counter-compony argent and sable
between three crosses pattée fitchée (untinctured). 2. Or, two bends gules.
3. Quarterly argent and or, three bars gules within a bordure sable charged with
ten fish haurient of the first. 4. Argent, an eagle displayed sable. 5. Azure,
three eagles displayed in bend between two bendlets engrailed argent.*

"No Armes in ye office Booke."

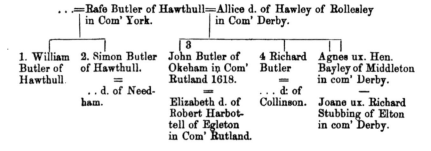

... =Rafe Butler of Hawthull=Allice d. of Hawley of Rollesley
| in Com' York. | in Com' Derby.

1. William   2. Simon Butler   3   4 Richard   Agnes ux. Hen.
Butler of   of Hawthull.   John Butler of   Butler   Bayley of Middleton
Hawthull.   =   Okeham in Com'   =   in com' Derby.
| .. d. of Need-   Rutland 1618.   ... d: of   —
| ham.   =   Collinson.   Joane ux. Richard
| Elizabeth d. of   Stubbing of Elton
| Robert Harbot-   in com' Derby.
| tell of Egleton
| in Com' Rutland.

(Mynne.)

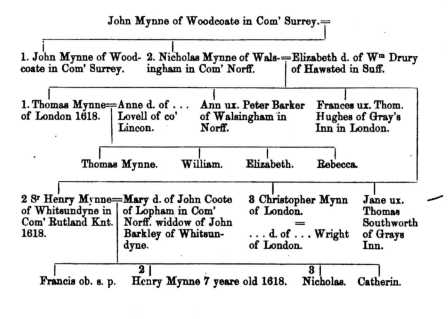

John Mynne of Woodcoate in Com' Surrey.=

1. John Mynne of Wood-
coate in Com' Surrey.

2. Nicholas Mynne of Wals-=Elizabeth d. of Wm Drury
ingham in Com' Norff. of Hawsted in Suff.

1. Thomas Mynne=Anne d. of . . .
of London 1618. Lovell of co'
Lincon.

Ann ux. Peter Barker
of Walsingham in
Norff.

Frances ux. Thom.
Hughes of Gray's
Inn in London.

Thomas Mynne. William. Elizabeth. Rebecca.

2 Sr Henry Mynne=Mary d. of John Coote
of Whitsundyne in of Lopham in Com'
Com' Rutland Knt. Norff. widdow of John
1618. Barkley of Whitsun-
dyne.

3 Christopher Mynn
of London.
=
. . . d. of . . . Wright
of London.

Jane ux.
Thomas
Southworth
of Grays
Inn.

Francis ob. s. p. 2 | Henry Mynne 7 yeare old 1618. 3 | Nicholas. Catherin.

(Booth.)

Hugh Booth of Cussington in Com'=Mary d. of Robert Harbottell
Lester Bachelor of Divinity. of Egleton in Com' Rutland.

John Booth of Okeham=Mary* d. of Bartin
in Com' Rutland sonne Burton of Okeham
& heire A° 1618. in Com' Rutland.

Elizabeth ux.
John Perpount
of Estwell in
Com' Lester.

Susan ux. Michill†
Wright of Brix-
worth in Com'
Northt.

* Mabel in Harl. 1094. † Nicho. in Harl. 1094.

Burton.

ARMS. *Sable, on a chevron between three owls argent, crowned or, a mullet for dif-*
ference (charged with a crescent, Harl. MS. 1094).
CREST. *An owl argent, crowned or.*

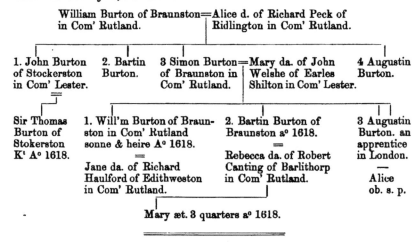

William Burton of Braunston=Alice d. of Richard Peck of
in Com' Rutland.   Ridlington in Com' Rutland.

1. John Burton   2. Bartin   3 Simon Burton=Mary da. of John   4 Augustin
of Stockerston   Burton.   of Braunston in | Welshe of Earles Burton.
in Com' Lester.   Com' Rutland. | Shilton in Com' Lester.

Sir Thomas   1. Will'm Burton of Braun-   2. Bartin Burton of   3 Augustin
Burton of   ston in Com' Rutland   Braunston a° 1618.   Burton. an
Stokerston   sonne & heire A° 1618.   apprentice
K* A° 1618.   =   in London.

                 Jane da. of Richard   Rebecca da. of Robert   —
                 Haulford of Edithweston   Canting of Barlithorp   Alice
                 in Com' Rutland.   in Com' Rutland.   ob. s. p.

        Mary æt. 3 quarters a° 1618.

(Houghton.)

ARMS. *Sable, three bars argent, in chief a rose or.*
CREST. *A bull's head argent, charged with three bars sable, on the upper one a rose or.*

A patent per Robert Cooke Clarenc. 1 Nouemb. 1584 26. Q. Eliz. To Toby
        Houghton of Kingscliff in Com' Northt. Esq.

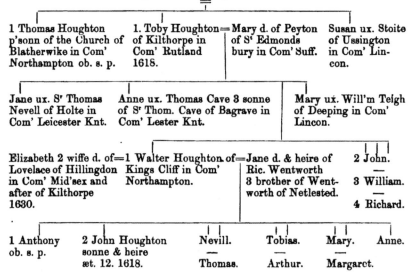

John Houghton of Kilthorpe in Com' Rutland.

1 Thomas Houghton   1. Toby Houghton=Mary d. of Peyton   Susan ux. Stoite
p'sonn of the Church of   of Kilthorpe in | of S* Edmonds   of Ussington
Blatherwike in Com'   Com' Rutland | bury in Com' Suff. in Com' Lin-
Northampton ob. s. p.   1618.   con.

Jane ux. S* Thomas   Anne ux. Thomas Cave 3 sonne   Mary ux. Will'm Teigh
Nevell of Holte in   of S* Thom. Cave of Bagrave in   of Deeping in Com'
Com' Leicester Knt.   Com' Lester Knt.   Lincon.

Elizabeth 2 wiffe d. of=1 Walter Houghton of=Jane d. & heire of   2 John.
Lovelace of Hillingdon Kings Cliff in Com' | Ric. Wentworth
in Com' Mid'sex and   Northampton. | 3 brother of Went-   3 William.
after of Kilthorpe | worth of Netlested.
1630.   4 Richard.

1 Anthony   2 John Houghton   Nevill.   Tobias.   Mary.   Anne.
ob. s. p.   sonne & heire   —   —   —
              æt. 12. 1618.   Thomas.   Arthur.   Margaret.

Welby.

ARMS. *Quarterly of six:*—1. *Sable, a fess between three fleurs-de-lis argent.*
WELBY. 2. *Barry of six argent and gules, in chief three roundels (untinc-
tured).* MOULTON. 3. *Or, a double-headed eagle, displayed sable pellettée.*
KINSEY al's SWALEY. 4. *Azure, a saltire between four cross crosslets or.*
FRISKNEY. 5. *Ermine, on a bend gules three leopards' heads or.* STYNT.

Richard Welby of Molton in Com' Lincon.=Anne d. & heire of Thomas Stint.

| 7. Roger Welby of Gedney in Com' Linc. = | 1. Richard vide Lincon. · = | 2. | 3 Miles occisus in Bella de blore s. p. — John a priest. | 4 Thomas Welby. = ... d. & h. of Sʳ Robt. Leake Kᵗ | 5 Robert a priest. — 6. William. |

Richard= ... d. of
Welby. | Thimelby.

Robert Welby ob. s. p.

Margaret.

Thomas. Agnes.

John Welby of Halsted in Com' Linc.

Richard Welby of Gedney
sonne & heire.
=
... sister of Henry Sutton
of Com' Notts.

Ellen da. of ... =2. Adlard Welby=Cassander da. of
Hall of Hall in | of Gedney in | Wᵐ Price of
Com' Ebor. 1 | Com' Lincon. | Washingley in
wife. | | Com' Hunting-
| | ton 2 wife.

Richard Welby.

Sir William Welby of Gedney Kᵗ of the Bath.

| Henry Welby of=Alice da. of Thom. White Gokeshill in of Tuxford in Com' Not-Com' Lincon. tingham sister of Eliza-beth. | Anne ux. Smith of Hadey in Com' Suff. | Jane ux. Thom. Ogle of Pinch-beck in Com' Lincoln. |

Elizabeth d. & heire ux. Sʳ Xprofer Hildyard of Holdernes Knt.

| Adlard Welby of Wood-=Elizabeth d. of Thom. head in the p'sh of Cas-White of Tuxford in terton in Com' Rutland Com' Nottingham 1618. sister of Allice. | Mary ux. Henry Adams of Tyd Sᵗ Marys in Holland. | Ellen ux. Cal-low of Hol-bech in Hol-land. |

| Friswide. | Mary ux. Wᵐ Burne of Man-chester in Com' Lank. Clerke. | Adlard Welby ob. s. p. — Henry Welby sonne & heire æt. 27 aᵒ 1618. | 2. Adlard Welby. | Elizabeth. — Rachell. | John ob. s. p. |

(Haddon.)

Robert Haddon of Braseburgh in Com' Lincon.

John Haddon of Braseburgh.

William Haddon of Essendine=Jane d. of Richard Wakefeld of
in Com' Rutland.   Castle Gresley in Com' Derby.

John Haddon of Essendine=Jane da. of James Naylor   Elizabeth ux. Richard
in Com' Rutland aº 1618.   of Essendyne.   Saunders of Sanford
                                                         in Com' Northampton.

William Haddon   2 John   Anne ux. Gabriell Boyall   Rose ux. Edward
sonne & heire   Haddon.   of Melstrop in Com'   Merry of Carlby
æt. 26 years aº 1618.   Rutland.   in Com' Lincon.

Joane ux. Thom.   2. Joseph Haddon=Elizabeth da. of   Jane ux. Richard
Humfrey of Easton   of Caysby in Com' Richard Durham   Harvye of Spalding
in Com' Lincon.   Lincon.   of Caysby.   in Com' Lincon.

1 John Haddon.   2 William Haddon.   Jane.   Elizabeth.

(Roos.)

ARMS. *Quarterly* :—1. *Azure, three water bougets or, a label of three points.* 2. *Or,
three lions rampant gules, a label of three points azure, sometimes argent.* 3.
Gules, a lion rampant vair, crowned or. (EVERINGHAM.) 4. *Barry of six
argent and gules, on a canton sable a cross flory of the first ; over all a crescent
for difference.* (ETTON.)

" No Armes in the Vissitation in the office but I have seene this for Roos of Ashwell.

Sᵣ Robert Roos, Lord of Igmanthorpe & Seeton &
many other mannors in Yorkshire.

Robert Roos eldest sonn=Elizabeth d. of Sᵣ John Midle-   William Roos 2 sonn
had Seeton.   ton of Midleton Hall.   had Igmanthorpe.

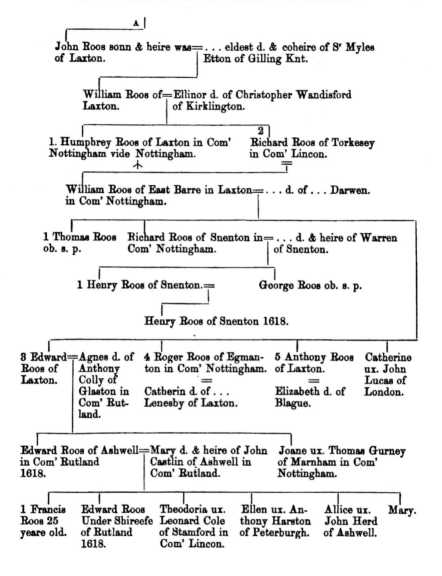

A |

John Roos sonn & heire was=... eldest d. & coheire of S' Myles
of Laxton.   Etton of Gilling Knt.

William Roos of=Ellinor d. of Christopher Wandisford
Laxton.   of Kirklington.

1. Humphrey Roos of Laxton in Com'   2 |
Nottingham vide Nottingham.   Richard Roos of Torkesey
                                 in Com' Lincon.

William Roos of East Barre in Laxton=... d. of ... Darwen.
in Com' Nottingham.

1 Thomas Roos   Richard Roos of Snenton in=... d. & heire of Warren
ob. s. p.   Com' Nottingham.   of Snenton.

1 Henry Roos of Snenton.=   George Roos ob. s. p.

Henry Roos of Snenton 1618.

3 Edward=Agnes d. of   4 Roger Roos of Egman-   5 Anthony Roos   Catherine
Roos of Anthony   ton in Com' Nottingham. of Laxton.   ux. John
Laxton. Colly of   =   =   Lucas of
         Glaston in   Catherin d. of ...   Elizabeth d. of London.
         Com' Rut-   Lenesby of Laxton.   Blague.
         land.

Edward Roos of Ashwell=Mary d. & heire of John   Joane ux. Thomas Gurney
in Com' Rutland   Castlin of Ashwell in   of Marnham in Com'
1618.   Com' Rutland.   Nottingham.

1 Francis   Edward Roos   Theodoria ux.   Ellen ux. An-   Allice ux.   Mary.
Roos 25   Under Shireefe Leonard Cole   thony Harston   John Herd
yeare old.   of Rutland   of Stamford in of Peterburgh. of Ashwell.
             1618.   Com' Lincon.

(Wilcox.)

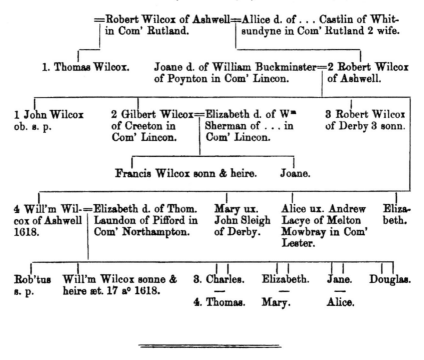

=Robert Wilcox of Ashwell=Allice d. of . . . Castlin of Whitin Com' Rutland.   sundyne in Com' Rutland 2 wife.

1. Thomas Wilcox.   Joane d. of William Buckminster=2 Robert Wilcox
of Poynton in Com' Lincon.   of Ashwell.

1 John Wilcox   2 Gilbert Wilcox=Elizabeth d. of W^m   3 Robert Wilcox
ob. s. p.   of Creeton in   Sherman of . . . in   of Derby 3 sonn.
     Com' Lincon.   Com' Lincon.

Francis Wilcox sonn & heire.   Joane.

4 Will'm Wil-=Elizabeth d. of Thom.   Mary ux.   Alice ux. Andrew   Eliza-
cox of Ashwell   Laundon of Pifford in   John Sleigh   Lacye of Melton   beth.
1618.   Com' Northampton.   of Derby.   Mowbray in Com'
          Lester.

Rob'tus   Will'm Wilcox sonne &   3. Charles.   Elizabeth.   Jane.   Douglas.
s. p.   heire æt. 17 aᵒ 1618.   —   —   —
          4. Thomas.   Mary.   Alice.

(Conny.)

ARMS. *Quarterly :—1. Gules, on a bend double cotised or, three torteaux. 2. Argent, two bars gemelles azure, in chief three mullets gules, over all a crescent for difference.*

CREST. *A talbot's head or, the tongue hanging out of his mouth, distilling blood proper, charged with a crescent for difference.*

"A patent per Will'm Segar Esq. alias Garter 2 June 1612 to Sʳ Thomas Conye of Basingthorpe in Com' Linc. Kᵗ.

"This coate and crest only without difference in the office visitation."

Robert Conny of Bayam in France came into England with=. . . d. of Sʳ John
Queene Issabell wife to King Edward the second.   Houltbeck.

Sir Hugh Conny, Knight.=Jane d. of Sʳ John
     Houldidg Knight.

A

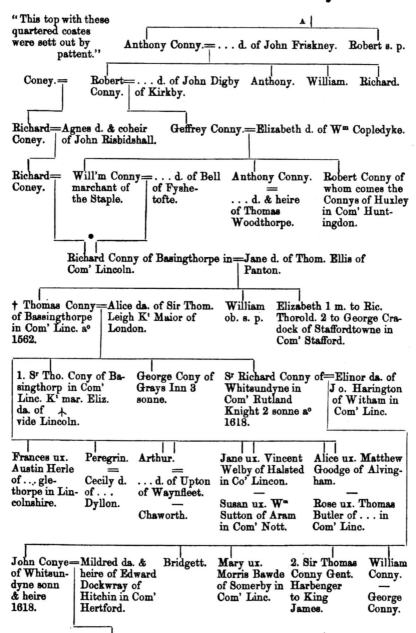

" This top with these quartered coates were sett out by pattent."

A

Anthony Conny.═ . . . d. of John Friskney.   Robert s. p.

Coney.═   Robert═ . . . d. of John Digby   Anthony.   William.   Richard.
           Conny.   of Kirkby.

Richard═Agnes d. & coheir   Geffrey Conny.═Elizabeth d. of Wᵐ Copledyke.
Coney.   of John Risbidshall.

Richard═   Will'm Conny═ . . . d. of Bell   Anthony Conny.   Robert Conny of
Coney.   marchant of   of Fyshe-   ═   whom comes the
           the Staple.   tofte.   . . . d. & heire   Connys of Huxley
                                          of Thomas   in Com' Hunt-
                                          Woodthorpe.   ingdon.

Richard Conny of Basingthorpe in═Jane d. of Thom. Ellis of
Com' Lincoln.   Panton.

† Thomas Conny═Alice da. of Sir Thom.   William   Elizabeth 1 m. to Ric.
of Bassingthorpe   Leigh Kᵗ Maior of   ob. s. p.   Thorold. 2 to George Cra-
in Com' Linc. aᵒ   London.   dock of Staffordtowne in
1562.   Com' Stafford.

1. Sʳ Tho. Cony of Ba-   George Cony of   Sʳ Richard Conny of═Elinor da. of
singthorp in Com'   Grays Inn 3   Whitsundyne in   J o. Harington
Linc. Kᵗ mar. Eliz.   sonne.   Com' Rutland   of Witham in
da. of A   Knight 2 sonne aᵒ   Com' Linc.
vide Lincoln.   1618.

Frances ux.   Peregrin.   Arthur.   Jane ux. Vincent   Alice ux. Matthew
Austin Herle   ═   ═   Welby of Halsted   Goodge of Alving-
of . . . gle-   Cecily d.   . . . d. of Upton   in Co' Lincon.   ham.
thorpe in Lin-   of . . .   of Waynfleet.   —   —
colnshire.   Dyllon.   —   Susan ux. Wᵐ   Rose ux. Thomas
                          Chaworth.   Sutton of Aram   Butler of . . . in
                                       in Com' Nott.   Com' Linc.

John Conye═Mildred da. &   Bridgett.   Mary ux.   2. Sir Thomas   William
of Whitsun-   heire of Edward   Morris Bawde   Conny Gent.   Conny.
dyne sonn   Dockwray of   of Somerby in   Harbenger   —
& heire   Hitchin in Com'   Com' Linc.   to King   George
1618.   Hertford.   James.   Conny.

Jane filia unica æt. dimid' anni t'p'e Visitaco'is.
This Coate and Crest only without difference in the office Visitation.

* Sic in MS.
† Harl. MS. 1094 commences with this Thomas, but does not mention his wife.

(Busby.)

ARMS. *Or, three bird-bolts sable, feathered argent, on a chief of the second as many mullets pierced of the field.*

CREST. *A stag's head erased argent, horned or, pierced through the neck from the back by an arrow of the first feathered gules.*

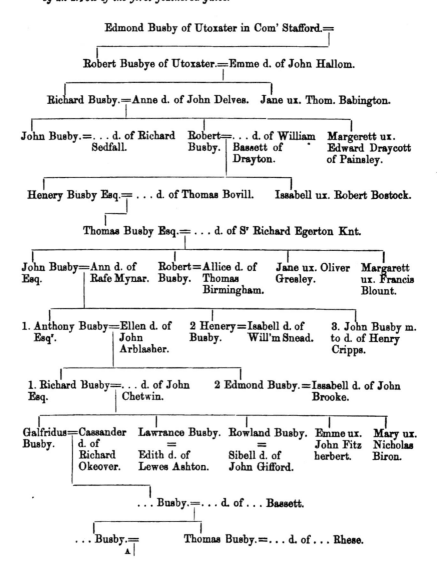

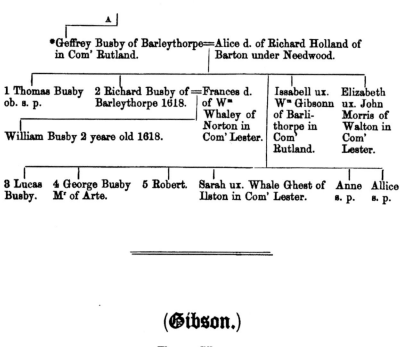

*Geffrey Busby of Barleythorpe=Alice d. of Richard Holland of
in Com' Rutland. Barton under Needwood.

1 Thomas Busby 2 Richard Busby of =Frances d. Issabell ux. Elizabeth
ob. s. p.   Barleythorpe 1618. of Wᵐ Wᵐ Gibsonn ux. John
                                      Whaley of of Barli- Morris of
William Busby 2 yeare old 1618.   Norton in thorpe in Walton in
                                      Com' Lester. Com' Com'
                                                 Rutland. Lester.

3 Lucas 4 George Busby 5 Robert. Sarah ux. Whale Ghest of Anne Allice
Busby.   Mʳ of Arte.   Ilston in Com' Lester.   s. p. s. p.

(Gibson.)

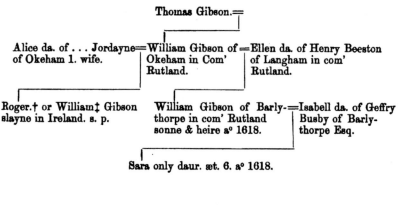

Thomas Gibson.=

Alice da. of . . . Jordayne=William Gibson of =Ellen da. of Henry Beeston
of Okeham 1. wife.   Okeham in Com' of Langham in com'
                            Rutland.   Rutland.

Roger.† or William‡ Gibson   William Gibson of Barly-=Isabell da. of Geffry
slayne in Ireland. s. p.   thorpe in com' Rutland Busby of Barly-
                             sonne & heire aᵒ 1618. thorpe Esq.

Sara only daur. æt. 6. aᵒ 1618.

---

* The pedigree in Harl. MS. 1094 begins here.
† Harl. MS. 1094.   ‡ Harl. MS. 1558.

(𝕵𝖔𝖍𝖓𝖘𝖔𝖓.)

ARMS. *Argent, a chevron sable between three lions' heads couped gules, crowned or.*
CREST. *A lion's head gules, ducally crowned or, between two ostrich feathers argent.*

"A patent by Robert Cooke Clar. 23 March 1592 35 Q. Eliz. to Rob. Johnson Batchiler in Divinity & Preacher of North Luffenham in Com' Rutland, Founder of two Gramer Schooles & two Hospitalls in Okeham and Upingham."

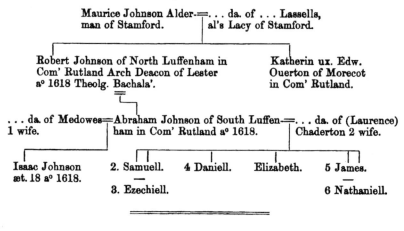

Maurice Johnson Alder- = . . . da. of . . . Lassells,
man of Stamford.   al's Lacy of Stamford.

Robert Johnson of North Luffenham in Com' Rutland Arch Deacon of Lester aº 1618 Theolg. Bachala'.

Katherin ux. Edw. Ouerton of Morecot in Com' Rutland.

. . . da. of Medowes = Abraham Johnson of South Luffenham in Com' Rutland aº 1618. = . . . da. of (Laurence) Chaderton 2 wife.
1 wife.

Isaac Johnson æt. 18 aº 1618.

2. Samuell.
—
3. Ezechiell.

4 Daniell.

Elizabeth.

5 James.
—
6 Nathaniell.

(𝕳𝖚𝖓𝖙.)

ARMS. *Quarterly :—1 and 4. Azure, a bend between six leopards' faces or.* (HUNT.)
   2 and 3. Argent, a fess sable between three garbs vert. (RIDOL.)
CREST. *A leopard's head between two wings expanded or.*

"A Patent of the first coate and creast to John Hunt of Lindon in com' Rutland, Esq. by Robert Cooke, Clar. 20 July, 1585. 27 Q. Elizabeth."

Another Quarterly : 1. HUNT. 2. (*Probably for* RIDOL.) 3. *Sable, a cross patonce ermine.* (DURANT.) 4. *Argent, a fess sable between three cocks' gules.* (   )

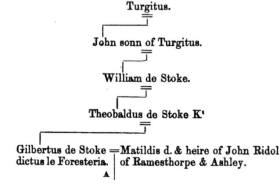

Turgitus.

John sonn of Turgitus.

William de Stoke.

Theobaldus de Stoke Kᵗ

Gilbertus de Stoke = Matildis d. & heire of John Ridol dictus le Foresteria.   of Ramesthorpe & Ashley.

A

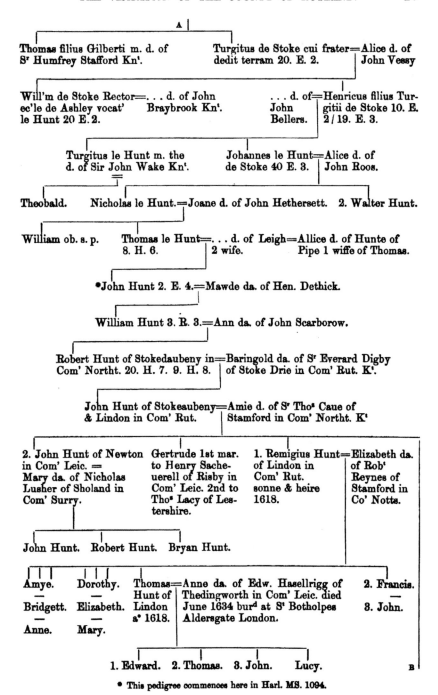

A

Thomas filius Gilberti m. d. of Sr Humfrey Stafford Kn^t.

Turgitus de Stoke cui frater=Alice d. of dedit terram 20. E. 2. | John Vessy

Will'm de Stoke Rector=. . . d. of John ec'le de Ashley vocat' Braybrook Kn^t. le Hunt 20 E. 2.

. . . d. of=Henricus filius Tur- John gitii de Stoke 10. E. Bellers. 2 / 19. E. 3.

Turgitus le Hunt m. the d. of Sir John Wake Kn^t.

Johannes le Hunt=Alice d. of de Stoke 40 E. 3. | John Roos.

Theobald. Nicholas le Hunt.=Joane d. of John Hethersett. 2. Walter Hunt.

William ob. s. p. Thomas le Hunt=. . . d. of Leigh=Allice d. of Hunte of 8. H. 6. 2 wife. Pipe 1 wiffe of Thomas.

*John Hunt 2. E. 4.=Mawde da. of Hen. Dethick.

William Hunt 3. R. 3.=Ann da. of John Scarborow.

Robert Hunt of Stokedaubeny in=Baringold da. of Sr Everard Digby Com' Northt. 20. H. 7. 9. H. 8. | of Stoke Drie in Com' Rut. K^t.

John Hunt of Stokeaubeny=Amie d. of Sr Thos Caue of & Lindon in Com' Rut. | Stamford in Com' Northt. K^t

2. John Hunt of Newton in Com' Leic. = Mary da. of Nicholas Lusher of Sholand in Com' Surry.

Gertrude 1st mar. to Henry Sache- uerell of Risby in Com' Leic. 2nd to Thos Lacy of Les- tershire.

1. Remigius Hunt=Elizabeth da. of Lindon in of Robt Com' Rut. Reynes of sonne & heire Stamford in 1618. Co' Notts.

John Hunt. Robert Hunt. Bryan Hunt.

Amye. — Bridgett. — Anne.

Dorothy. — Elizabeth. — Mary.

Thomas=Anne da. of Edw. Hasellrigg of Hunt of | Thedingworth in Com' Leic. died Lindon | June 1634 bur^d at St Botholpes a^o 1618. | Aldersgate London.

2. Francis. — 3. John.

1. Edward. 2. Thomas. 3. John. Lucy.

B

* This pedigree commences here in Harl. MS. 1094.

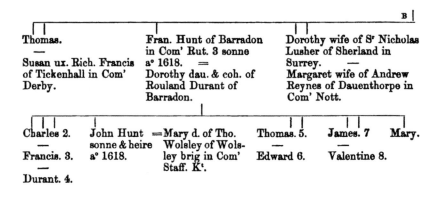

B |

Thomas.	Fran. Hunt of Barradon in Com' Rut. 3 sonne aº 1618. =	Dorothy wife of Sr Nicholas Lusher of Sherland in Surrey.
—	Dorothy dau. & coh. of	—
Susan ux. Rich. Francis of Tickenhall in Com' Derby.	Rouland Durant of Barradon.	Margaret wife of Andrew Reynes of Dauenthorpe in Com' Nott.

Charles 2.	John Hunt sonne & heire aº 1618.	=Mary d. of Tho. Wolsley of Wolsley brig in Com' Staff. Kt.	Thomas. 5.	James. 7	Mary.
—			—		
Francis. 3.			Edward 6.	Valentine 8.	
—					
Durant. 4.					

(Overton.)

ARMS. *Quarterly :—1 and 4. Argent, a cross formée gules.* (OVERTON.) *2. Or, an eagle displayed azure, armed and beaked gules.* (MONGOMERY.) *3. Sable, on a chevron between three suns in their splendour argent, a crescent of the field for difference.* (EDWELL.)

CREST. *A maiden's head proper, vested and wreathed gules, crined or.*

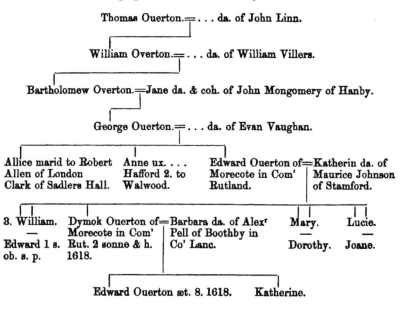

Thomas Ouerton.=. . . da. of John Linn.

William Overton.=. . . da. of William Villers.

Bartholomew Overton.=Jane da. & coh. of John Mongomery of Hanby.

George Ouerton.=. . . da. of Evan Vaughan.

| Allice marid to Robert Allen of London Clark of Sadlers Hall. | Anne ux. . . . Hafford 2. to Walwood. | Edward Ouerton of Morecote in Com' Rutland. | =Katherin da. of Maurice Johnson of Stamford. |

3. William.	Dymok Ouerton of Morecote in Com' Rut. 2 sonne & h. 1618.	=Barbara da. of Alexr Pell of Boothby in Co' Lanc.	Mary.	Lucie.
—			—	—
Edward 1 s. ob. s. p.			Dorothy.	Joane.

Edward Ouerton æt. 8. 1618.   Katherine.

(Digby.)

ARMS. *Quarterly :—*1 *and* 4. *Azure, a fleur-de-lis argent.* (DIGBY.) 2 *and* 3. *Gules, a chevron between three cross crosslets fitchée argent.* (PAKEMAN.)

Robert Digby of Tilson=Catherine d. & coheire of Simon Pake-=Thomas Seyton
in Com' Lester. man of Kirby & Wigtone. 2 husband.

Symon al's Everard Digby=Agnes d. of John=Richard Seddall
of Tilton. Clark. 1 husband.

Sir Everard Digby of Tilton in=Jaquet d. of Sr John Ellis
Com' Lester Knt. of Com' Devon.

1 Sr Everard Digby 3. Sir John Digby of Eye=Catherine da. of Nicholas
sonne & heire. Kettleby in Com' Leic. Griffin of Braybrook in Co'
人 Kt 3. sonne. Northampton.

Symon Digby 2=Catherin da. of Clapham William Digby.
sonne. of Beamesley Co. York. 人

Roger Digby of North=Mary da. of John Cheney of Sherd- 1. Augustin
Luffenham in Com' loes in the parish of Agmondisham Digby.
Rutland 2 sonne. in Com' Buck.

Katherin da. of=James Digby of North Luffenham=Ann. d. & h. of Partrich
Kenelin Digby Esq. sonne & heir 1618. of Co Linc. Widow of
of Stoke Dry = Wm Brudenell 5. son of
in Com' Rut- 3rdly Benedic da. of Skinner of Sir Thos Brudenell
land 1 wife. the County of Warwick widdow 2 wife.
 of Wednester.

John Digby sonne=Mary d. of Rich. Martyn Ursula ux. George
& heire ao of Long Melford in Clifford of Brakenburgh
1618. Com' Suff. in Com' Linc.
 =

James eld. son. Alice æt. 1. Ursula.

D

(Osborne.)

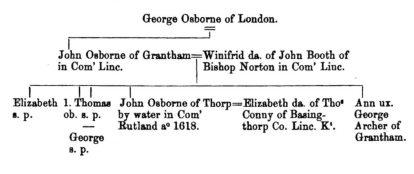

George Osborne of London.

John Osborne of Grantham=Winifrid da. of John Booth of
in Com' Linc. | Bishop Norton in Com' Linc.

Elizabeth s. p.	1. Thomas ob. s. p.	John Osborne of Thorp=Elizabeth da. of Tho⁵	Ann ux.
	— George s. p.	by water in Com' Rutland aᵒ 1618.	Conny of Basingthorp Co. Linc. Kᵗ.	George Archer of Grantham.

Bassett.

ARMS. *Argent, three bars dancettee gules.*

"This coate is tricked in black lead by the other in the office Book."

ARMS. *Or, three piles meeting in base gules, a canton vair.*

Thomas Bassett of North Luffenham in com' Rutland.=

John Bassett of North Luffenham.=Ann da. of . . . Rowse of Rowflinch
in Com' Worcester.

John Bassett of North Luffenham=Eliz. da. of Gregory (or George)* Lyon
Aᵒ 1618. | de com' Linc.

| 2. Francis. — 3. Edward. — 4. George. — 5. Nicholas. | Ann ux. Thomas Herenden of Barkworth in Co' Linc. | John Basse of Eastriche in Com' Lincoln Aᵒ 1618. | =Ann da. & h. of Kirkman of Easterkel in Com' Linc. | Wiburg ux. Evan Hunt of North Luffenham. | Thomas — James ob. s. p. | Audrey. — Elizabeth. — Sara. — Barbara. |

Kirkham Bassett æt. 2. 1618.   Amie.

* Harl. MS. 1094.

𝔖𝔥𝔢𝔣𝔣𝔢𝔩𝔡.

ARMS. *Quarterly* :—1 and 4. *Or, a fess between six garbs gules.* (SHEFFELD.)
  2 and 3. *Argent, two bars and in chief three fleurs-de-lis gules.* (St. LIS.)

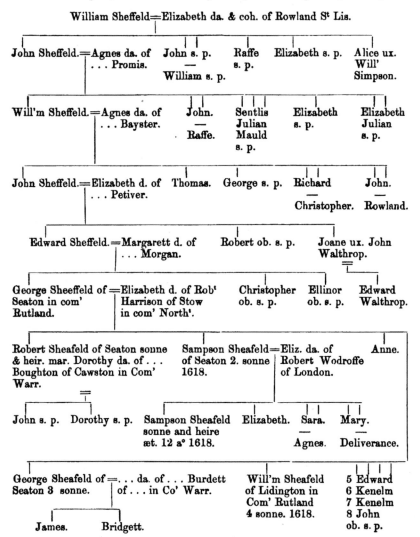

William Sheffeld=Elizabeth da. & coh. of Rowland St Lis.

John Sheffeld.=Agnes da. of | John s. p. | Raffe s. p. | Elizabeth s. p. | Alice ux. Will' Simpson.
... Promis. | — William s. p.

Will'm Sheffeld.=Agnes da. of | John. — Raffe. | Sentlis Julian Mauld s. p. | Elizabeth s. p. | Elizabeth Julian s. p.
... Bayster.

John Sheffeld.=Elizabeth d. of | Thomas. | George s. p. | Richard — Christopher. | John. — Rowland.
... Petiver.

Edward Sheffeld.=Margarett d. of | Robert ob. s. p. | Joane ux. John Walthrop.
... Morgan.

George Sheeffeld of =Elizabeth d. of Robt | Christopher ob. s. p. | Ellinor ob. s. p. | Edward Walthrop.
Seaton in com' | Harrison of Stow
Rutland. | in com' North'.

Robert Sheafeld of Seaton sonne & heir. mar. Dorothy da. of ... Boughton of Cawston in Com' Warr. | Sampson Sheafeld = Eliz. da. of of Seaton 2. sonne | Robert Wodroffe 1618. | of London. | Anne.

John s. p. | Dorothy s. p. | Sampson Sheafeld sonne and heire æt. 12 aᵒ 1618. | Elizabeth. | Sara. — Agnes. | Mary. Deliverance.

George Sheafeld of =... da. of ... Burdett Seaton 3 sonne. | of ... in Co' Warr. | Will'm Sheafeld of Lidington in Com' Rutland 4 sonne. 1618. | 5 Edward 6 Kenelm 7 Kenelm 8 John ob. s. p.

James. | Bridgett.

Noate y^t in y^e vissitation in y^e office this descent beginneth with ¶ George that marid w'th Elizabeth Harrisson and all ye descents above him weare taken out of a very auntiant Rowle in w'ch Rowle y^e Coate of Sheffeld was set out in Collers as it is aboue tricked viz. fflower de luces in sted of Garbes neither is there in the sayd Vissitation that brother & sister of George viz. Christopher & Ellynor who both dyed without issue.

(Digby.)

Sir Everard Digby of Tilton in co' Leic. Kt.=. . . Jaquet.

Sir Everard Digby sonne=Margery da. of Sir John Hey-   Sᵣ John Digby of Eye
& heir Kᵗ.   don of . . . co' Norfolk Kᵗ.   Kettleby Kᵗ 3ᵈ sonne.

Kenelyn Digby of Stoke=Ann da. of Sir Anthony Coope of   vide p. 17.
sonne & heire.   Hanwell in com' Oxon. Kᵗ.

1. Everard Digby=Mary da. & coh. of Francis=Sampson Erdeswick of Sandon
sonne & heire.   Neale of Kethorpe in   in com' Stafford (1ˢᵗ husb.).
                 com' Leic.

1. Sᵣ Everard=Mary da. & h.   2. George.   Mary ux.   Elizabeth.   Richard
Digby Kᵗ   of Will'm   —   Sᵣ Robᵗ   Erdes-
attainted Aº Mulsho of   3. John.   Wright al's   wick.
(3) King   Goathurst in   Reeve of Thwayte
James.   co. Bucks.   in com' Suff.

Sᵣ Keneln Digby Kᵗ of Gotherst=Venetia da. & coh. of Sᵣ Edward   2. John
in Com' Bucks.   Stanley of Winwick in com' Oxon   Digby.
                               Kᵗ of the Bath.

Kenelme Digby.

Anthony Digby   . . . d. of . . . Palmer=*John Digby of Seaton=Thomasin da. of
of Aston.   of . . . in Com'   in Com' Rutland Esq.   . . . 2 wife.
ob. s. p.   Leic. 1 wife.   1618.

Ann wife of Thomas Swinglehurst   Ursula.   Kenelin Digby   2. James   Mary.
of Seaton in Com' Rutland.   20 years old   Digby.   —
                                            1618.   Elizabeth.

* *Note.*—According to Harl. MS. 1094, the children of John Digby should change places of the
    wives; but they are given as above in the Visitation in the College of Arms.

(Cheselden.)

(See Addenda, p. 50.)

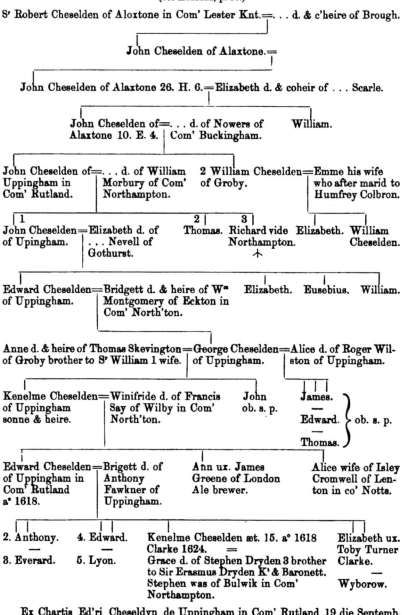

S[r] Robert Cheselden of Aloxtone in Com' Lester Knt.=. . . d. & c'heire of Brough.

John Cheselden of Alaxtone.=

John Cheselden of Alaxtone 26. H. 6.=Elizabeth d. & coheir of . . . Scarle.

John Cheselden of=. . . d. of Nowers of William.
Alaxtone 10. E. 4. | Com' Buckingham.

John Cheselden of=. . . d. of William   2 William Cheselden=Emme his wife
Uppingham in | Morbury of Com'   of Groby. | who after marid to
Com' Rutland. | Northampton. | Humfrey Colbron.

1
John Cheselden=Elizabeth d. of   2 | 3 |
of Upingham. | . . . Nevell of   Thomas. Richard vide Elizabeth. William
| Gothurst. | Northampton. Cheselden.

Edward Cheselden=Bridgett d. & heire of W[m]   Elizabeth. Eusebius. William.
of Uppingham. | Montgomery of Eckton in
| Com' North'ton.

Anne d. & heire of Thomas Skevington=George Cheselden=Alice d. of Roger Wil-
of Groby brother to S[r] William 1 wife. | of Uppingham. | ston of Uppingham.

Kenelme Cheselden=Winifride d. of Francis   John   James.
of Uppingham | Say of Wilby in Com'   ob. s. p. | —
sonne & heire. | North'ton. | Edward. } ob. s. p.
| —
| Thomas.

Edward Cheselden=Brigett d. of   Ann ux. James   Alice wife of Isley
of Uppingham in | Anthony   Greene of London Cromwell of Len-
Com' Rutland | Fawkner of   Ale brewer. ton in co' Notts.
a° 1618. | Uppingham.

2. Anthony.   4. Edward.   Kenelme Cheselden æt. 15. a° 1618   Elizabeth ux.
—   —   Clarke 1624.   =   Toby Turner
3. Everard.   5. Lyon.   Grace d. of Stephen Dryden 3 brother Clarke.
to Sir Erasmus Dryden K[t] & Baronett. | —
Stephen was of Bulwik in Com'   Wyborow.
Northampton.

Ex Chartis Ed'ri Cheseldyn de Uppingham in Com' Rutland 19 die Septemb. 1618.

Omnibus hoc scriptum visuris vel audituris Hugo filius Henrici de Uppingham salutem in d'no. Nouerit universitas v'ra me dedisse d'no Steph'o de Neuille unam p'tem bosci mei in bosco de Beumund sicut metæ circundant inter boscum d'ni Petri de Monteforti ex una, et bosc' Simonis de Sc'o Lycio quondam ex alia &c. Hiis testibus D'nis Henrico Murdach, Rad'o de Bella fago militibus Joh'e de Offinton, Petro de Hamule et aliis.

Sachent totez gentz nous Piers de Mountford Seigneur de Badesert avoir lesse a Thomas Fitz Tebaud de Ouderby la gard del corps Margerie fil et heir Will'm' Verder de Uppingham ensemblem¹ ou le mariage la dite Margerie &c. Escript a Whitchurch Ano. 26. E. 3.

Sciant p'sentes et futuri quod ego Joh'es Cheselden senior dedi Mauritio Lyney, Thomæ Morgan, Rob'to Chesilden et Nich'o Baxster 8 mess. septem virg. t'ræ cum p'tin in Braunston in Com' Rotel. Habendum eis et heredibus et asigneor' in p'ptm. Hiis testibus Joh'e Boyuile de Stoke i Faston, Thoma Flore de Okeham, Armigeris et aliis. Dat apud Braunston 7 de Septemb. A⁰ 6. E. 4.

Sciant p'ntes et futuri quod ego Joh'es Chesilden de Uppingham. Ar. dedi Henrico duci Buck, Ed'ro Comiti Wilts, Militibus Georgio Hopton, Rob'to Harington, Joh'i Sotehill, Thomæ Nevill, Rob'to Sotehill, Ric'o Boyvyle, Armigeris W⁰ Sheffeld et Joh'i Walle heredibus et assign' eor' in p'pt'm manerium meum de Lye cum omnibus suis p'tin in com' Rotl. ac costodiam ballivor forestæ Rotl' cum proficiis &c. Hiis testibus Henrico Sotehill de Stoke Faston seniore, Briano Talbot de Exton, Will'o Boyuill de Ridlington Armigeris et aliis. Dat. 8⁰ Septemb. Ano. 1. R. 3.

(Seal within a garter.) A chevron between three crosses anchorée.

Sciant p'ntes et futuri quod nos Mauritius Lyney, Thom. Morgan, Rob'tus Cheselden et Nich'us Baxster dimisimus Joh'i Chesilden juniori et Elizabethæ uxori ejus 8 mess' septem virg' t'ræ &c. in Braunston in Co. Rotl. quæ nuper h'uimus de dono Joh'is Chesilden senioris &c. Dat. 23 Septembris A⁰ 6. E. 4.

```
Johannes Chesilden senior.=
         |
    _____
   |
Johannes Chesilden junior.=Elizabetha uxor ejus A⁰ 6. E. 4.
```

Nouerint universi p' p'sentes nos Joh'em Chesilden de Adloxton seniorem Armigerum Joh'em Chesilden de Upingham juniorem gentilman et Will'm Chesilden de Adloxton gentilman teneri Joh'i Robert de Leicestre in centum m'cis sterlingor' &c. Dat. A⁰ 10 E. 4.

Omnibus xpi fidelibus &c. noveritis me Rob'tum Merbury filium W'i Merbury armigeri ad vsum et intenconem quandem indenturam fact' inter Franciscum Aynesworth et Eliz. Mongomery nuper uxorem Will'i Mongomery de Ekton in Co. North'ton armigeri defuncti ex una p'te et me prefatum Rob'tum Merbury et Edwardum Chesilden ex altera p'te gerent' dat. 16 Feb. A⁰ 6. H. 8 tradidi dimissi &c. Edmundo Haselwood et aliis omnia illa maneria terr' et tenta in Upingham et Braunston &c. ad opus et usum Ed'i Cheselden et Brigittæ uxori suæ uni filiar' p'd'ci Will'mi Mongomery et heredibus de corpore dicti Ed'i &c. remanere Euseby Cheselden f'ri p'di Ed'ri &c. remanere Will'o Chesilden f'ri p'dci, Ed'i &c. remanere Elizabeth Chesiiden sorori dicto Ed'ri. Dat. p'mo die Maii 7. H. 8.

```
Chesilden.=      Willemus Montgomeri defunctus=Elizabetha Aynesworth
     |            A⁰ 7. H. 8.                   |  A⁰ 7. H. 8.
  ___|_____        |
 |            |            |          |         |
Eusebius   Willimus    Elizabetha.  Edwardus=Brigitta una filiarum.
Chesilden. Chesilden.                Chesilden.
```

An indenture of mariage betweene Thomas* Skeffington of Groby in Com' Leic. thelder & Edward Chesilden of Uppingham in Com' Rotl. gent. That George Chesilden sonn & heire apparant of the sayd Edward shall take to wife Ann Skeffington daughter of the sayd George* before Michelmas A⁰ 1537 the indenture bearing date A⁰ 27. H. 8 the 28th of May.

* Sic.

(Walcot.)

Simon Walcot of Swaton = Alice d. of . . . Sharpe of
in Com' Lincoln.   Gunnerby in Com' Lincoln.

Robert (or Richard)* Walcote of Uppingham = Katherine da. of John Burton
in Com' Rutland sonne & heire aᵒ 1618.   of Stokerston in Com' Leic.

Thomas Walcot sonne & heire æt. 21. aᵒ 1618.	Patientia s. p.	Katherine. Ann.	Elizabeth. Frances.	Jane. Mary.	Abigall. Mabel.

Henry Walcot of Hel- = . . . d. of Launcelott Car of   Anne ux. John Midleton of
pringham in Com' Linc.   Sleaford in Com' Linc.   Swaton in Com' Linc.

Launcelott Walcott.

(Kay.)

Arms. *Argent, two bends sable.*

Arthur Kay of Woodsom = Beatrix da. of Matthew
in Com' Ebor.   Wentworth of Bretton.

John Kay of Woodsom = Dorothe da. of Sʳ Christ. Maleuerer
sonn & heire.   of Arnecliff in com' Ebor. Kᵗ.

1 Robert Kay of = Anne da. of John   **2.** Arthur Kay of = Ellin da. of Hipolie
Woodsam.   Flower of Whitwell   Hackney in   Lennett widow of
in Com' Rutland.   Com' Middx.   Welshe.

John Kay of = Elizabeth da. of Sʳ John Ferne   1. Arthur.   3. Peter.
Woodsam.   of . . . in Com' Linc. Kᵗ.   2. Francis.   4. Paul.

Anne da. of = Richard Kaye = Mary da. of John   **4.** Edward Kay = Beatrix da.
James Speght   of Edith Wes-   Flower of Whitwell   of Staveley   of Nevell of
of Ely in   ton in Com'   relict of John Calde-   in Com'   Ragnell in
Com' Cantab.   Rutland 1618.   cott of Ketton.   Derby.   Com' Nott.
1 wife.   2. wife.

James Kay æt. 30 aᵒ 1618.	**2** John Kay.	Ann ux. Isack Inman of Pinchbeck in co' Lincoln.	Richard Caldecott.	1. Nevell.	2. Peter. 3. John.

* Harl. MS. 1094.

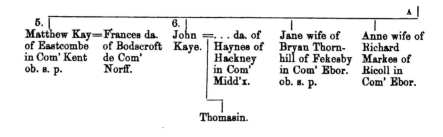

5.
Matthew Kay=Frances da.
of Eastcombe of Bodscroft
in Com' Kent de Com'
ob. s. p. Norff.

6.
John =... da. of
Kaye. | Haynes of
| Hackney
| in Com'
| Midd'x.

Jane wife of
Bryan Thorn-
hill of Fekesby
in Com' Ebor.
ob. s. p.

A |
Anne wife of
Richard
Markes of
Ricoll in
Com' Ebor.

Thomasin.

(Palmer.)

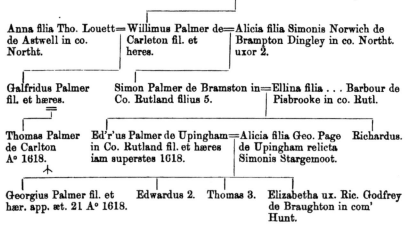

Tho. Palmer de Carlton in Com' Northt.=Katherina filia . . . Conyers.

Anna filia Tho. Louett=Willimus Palmer de=Alicia filia Simonis Norwich de
de Astwell in co. | Carleton fil. et | Brampton Dingley in co. Northt.
Northt. | heres. | uxor 2.

Galfridus Palmer   Simon Palmer de Bramston in=Ellina filia . . . Barbour de
fil. et hæres.   Co. Rutland filius 5. | Pisbrooke in co. Rutl.

Thomas Palmer   Ed'r'us Palmer de Upingham=Alicia filia Geo. Page   Richardus.
de Carlton   in Co. Rutland fil. et hæres | de Upingham relicta
A° 1618.   iam superstes 1618. | Simonis Stargemoot.

Georgius Palmer fil. et   Edwardus 2.   Thomas 3.   Elizabetha ux. Ric. Godfrey
hær. app. æt. 21 A° 1618.   de Braughton in com'
                                                        Hunt.

(Halford.)

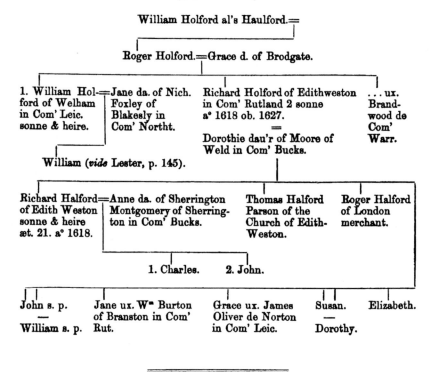

William Holford al's Haulford.=

Roger Holford.=Grace d. of Brodgate.

1. William Hol-=Jane da. of Nich.
ford of Welham Foxley of
in Com' Leic.   Blakesly in
sonne & heire. Com' Northt.

William (*vide* Lester, p. 145).

Richard Holford of Edithweston
in Com' Rutland 2 sonne
aº 1618 ob. 1627.
=
Dorothie dau'r of Moore of
Weld in Com' Bucks.

... ux.
Brand-
wood de
Com'
Warr.

Richard Halford=Anne da. of Sherrington
of Edith Weston Montgomery of Sherring-
sonne & heire   ton in Com' Bucks.
æt. 21. aº 1618.

Thomas Halford
Parson of the
Church of Edith-
Weston.

Roger Halford
of London
merchant.

1. Charles.   2. John.

John s. p.   Jane ux. Wᵐ Burton   Grace ux. James   Susan.   Elizabeth.
—   of Branston in Com'   Oliver de Norton   —
William s. p.   Rut.   in Com' Leic.   Dorothy.

(Colly.)

ARMS. *Quarterly*:—1. *Argent, a cross wavy sable.* 2. *Barry undée of six argent
and sable, on a canton gules a crescent or.* (KEBELL.)
CREST. *A griffon segreant argent, armed or.*

John Colly of Lubenham in=... sister of Sʳ John
Com. Lester.   Harington Knt.

John Colly of Lubenham.

William Colly of Glaston in Com' Rutland.=Anne d. of
...

John Colly of Glaston.=Issabell d. of Will'm Palmer of Carlton
in Com. Northampton.

A

E

A |

Catherin d. of Sr Wm Skeffing-=Anthony Colly of=Julian daughter of Cutbert
ton of Skeffington Com. | Glaston in Com. | Richardson of Com. York
Lester Knt. 1 wiffe. | Rutland. | 2 wife.

Margery ux. Dorothy Mary   ...ux. Anthony ...ux. Miles Mary ux. Ed-
John Flower ux. John ux.   Andrewes of   Forest of   ward Forrest of
of Whitwell Dark-   Pisbrooke in   Peter-   Middleham
in Com. Rut- nall.   Rutland.   borough.   Park in Com'
land.   York.

Anne ux. 1 Anthony=Elizabeth d. & heire 2. John Colby=Bridgett d. & co-
John   Colly of | of Henry Keble   of Glaston | heire of Cutbert
Withers   Glaston | of Humberstone in   ob. s. p. | Beuercotts of
of Lon-   in Com' | Com. Lester. | Beuercotts in Com'
don.   Rutland.   Nottingham.

Anthony Colly=Anne d. of Wi'm   Elizabeth ux. Rich- Jane. Anne ux. John
of Glaston in | Turpin of Knap- ard King of Ashley   King of Somon-
Com' Rutland | tofte in Com'   in Com' Lincon.   by in Com'
1618. | Lester.   Lincon.

Will'm Colby 2 yeare old 1618.   Anne.   Elizabeth.

"Here ends the Visitation made in A° 1618."

THE FOLLOWING PEDIGREES ARE NOT INCLUDED IN HARL. MS. No. 1094.

(𝕻𝖊𝖈𝖐.)

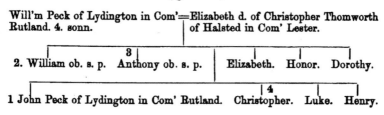

Will'm Peck of Lydington in Com'=Elizabeth d. of Christopher Thomworth Rutland. 4. sonn. | of Halsted in Com' Lester.

2. William ob. s. p.   3 Anthony ob. s. p.   Elizabeth.   Honor.   Dorothy.

1 John Peck of Lydington in Com' Rutland.   Christopher.   Luke.   Henry.

(𝕹𝖊𝖉𝖍𝖆𝖒.)*

ARMS. *Argent, a bend engrailed azure, between two bucks' heads cabossed sable.*
CREST. *On a mound vert, a stag lodged sable, attired or.*

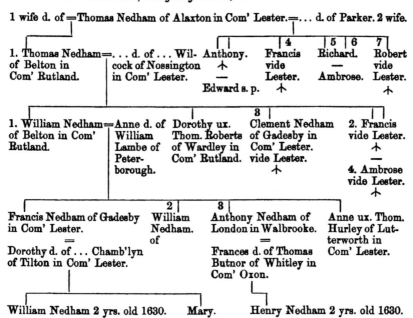

1 wife d. of = Thomas Nedham of Alaxton in Com' Lester. = ... d. of Parker. 2 wife.

1. Thomas Nedham = ... d. of ... Wil-   Anthony.   4 Francis   5 6 Richard.   7 Robert
of Belton in   cock of Nossington   vide   —   vide
Com' Rutland.   in Com' Lester.   Edward s. p.   Lester.   Ambrose.   Lester.

1. William Nedham = Anne d. of   Dorothy ux.   3 Clement Nedham   2. Francis
of Belton in Com'   William   Thom. Roberts   of Gadesby in   vide Lester.
Rutland.   Lambe of   of Wardley in   Com' Lester.   4. Ambrose
  Peter-   Com' Rutland.   vide Lester.   vide Lester.
  borough.

Francis Nedham of Gadesby   2 William   3 Anthony Nedham of   Anne ux. Thom.
in Com' Lester.   Nedham.   London in Walbrooke.   Hurley of Lut-
=   of   =   terworth in
Dorothy d. of ... Chamb'lyn   Frances d. of Thomas   Com' Lester.
of Tilton in Com' Lester.   Butnor of Whitley in
   Com' Oxon.

William Nedham 2 yrs. old 1630.   Mary.   Henry Nedham 2 yrs. old 1630.

---

* For many additions to this pedigree, see 'Visitation of Leicestershire,' Harl. Soc. Pub. vol. ii. page 100.

(𝕸ettenhall.)

ARMS. *Quarterly :—1 and 4. Vert, a bend ermine.* (WETTENHALL *ancient.*) 2 *and*
  3. *Vert, a cross engrailed ermine.* (WETTENHALL *modern.*)
CREST. *An antelope's head argent, attired or, issuing out of a ducal coronet gules.*

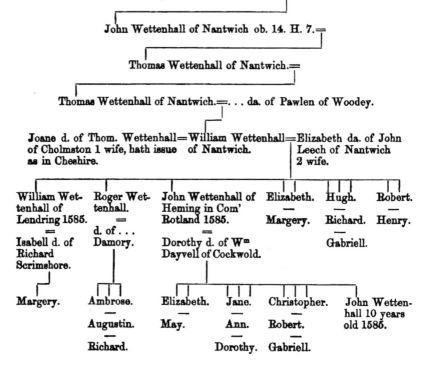

John Wettenhall of Nantwich in Com' Chester 23. H. 6.=Alice d. of . . . ob. 4. H. 7.

John Wettenhall of Nantwich ob. 14. H. 7.=

Thomas Wettenhall of Nantwich.=

Thomas Wettenhall of Nantwich.=. . . da. of Pawlen of Woodey.

Joane d. of Thom. Wettenhall=William Wettenhall=Elizabeth da. of John
of Cholmston 1 wife, hath issue   of Nantwich.   Leech of Nantwich
as in Cheshire.   2 wife.

William Wet-   Roger Wet-   John Wettenhall of   Elizabeth.   Hugh.   Robert.
tenhall of   tenhall.   Heming in Com'   —   —   —
Lendring 1585. =   Rotland 1585.   Margery.   Richard.   Henry.
=   d. of . . .   —
Isabell d. of Damory.   =   Gabriell.
Richard   Dorothy d. of Wm
Scrimshore.   Dayvell of Cockwold.

Margery.   Ambrose.   Elizabeth.   Jane.   Christopher.   John Wetten-
               —   —   —   —   hall 10 years
               Augustin.   May.   Ann.   Robert.   old 1585.
               —   —
               Richard.   Dorothy.   Gabriell.

Broughton.

ARMS. *Quarterly of six :—1 and 6. Argent, two bars gules, on a canton of the second
  a cross of the field.* (BROUGHTON.) 2. *Argent, a stag's head cabossed gules, a
  chief sable.* 3. *Or, on a fess azure three mullets of the field.* 4. *Argent, a
  chevron rompu between three trefoils slipped sable.* 5. *Argent, two bars and a
  canton gules, over all a bend azure ; over all a crescent for difference.*
CREST. *A sea-dog's head gules, a crescent for difference.*

John Broughton of Broughton=Margarett d. & sole heire of Allan Copland
tower in Furnes in Com' | Knt descended from the lord Copland's
Lanck. | house of Egremont.

A

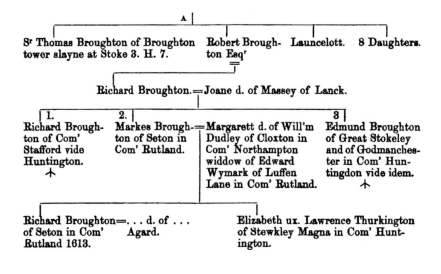

A |

Sʳ Thomas Broughton of Broughton tower slayne at Stoke 3. H. 7.   Robert Brough-ton Esqʳ   Launcelott.   8 Daughters.

Richard Broughton.═Joane d. of Massey of Lanck.

1. Richard Brough-ton of Com' Stafford vide Huntington.

2. Markes Brough-ton of Seton in Com' Rutland.═Margarett d. of Will'm Dudley of Cloxton in Com' Northampton widdow of Edward Wymark of Luffen Lane in Com' Rutland.

3 Edmund Broughton of Great Stokeley and of Godmanches-ter in Com' Hun-tingdon vide idem.

Richard Broughton═. . . d. of . . . of Seton in Com' Rutland 1613.   Agard.

Elizabeth ux. Lawrence Thurkington of Stewkley Magna in Com' Hunt-ington.

(Flower.)

ARMS. *Quarterly of eight:—1 and 8. Ermines, a cinquefoil ermine.* (FLOWER.) *2. Argent, a bend engrailed and a canton sable.* (DALBYE.) *3. Ermine, on a bend sable three quatrefoils argent.* (SALTEBYE.) *4. Sable, a chevron vair between three leopards' heads erased or.* (TANSLEY.) *5. Argent, a chevron between three eagles displayed gules.* (FRAUNCES.) *6. Azure, a cross flory between four martlets argent.* (PLESSINGTON.) *7. Gules, a chevron vair between six mullets or.* (TESSINGTON.)
CREST. *A flower ermine, foliated vert.*

William Flower.═   Sʳ Robert Plessington Knt. Threasurer of the Exchequer.═

Will'm Flower high shireeff of Rutland 10. R. 2.═   John Tansley.═   Rob. Plessington Esq.═

Roger Flower.═Catharin d. & coheire of Wᵐ Dalby of Exton in com' Rutland.   Peter Saltby═. . . d. & of Com' heire of Lincon. John.   **2** John Ples-sington of Burley.═   **1** Sʳ Henery Plessing-ton.═

Thomas═Agnes d. & heire Flower. of Peter Saltbie.   Sir John═Issabell d. Fraunces & coheire. Knight.   William Ples-═. . . d. sington ob. Lord s. p. Scroope.

A | B |

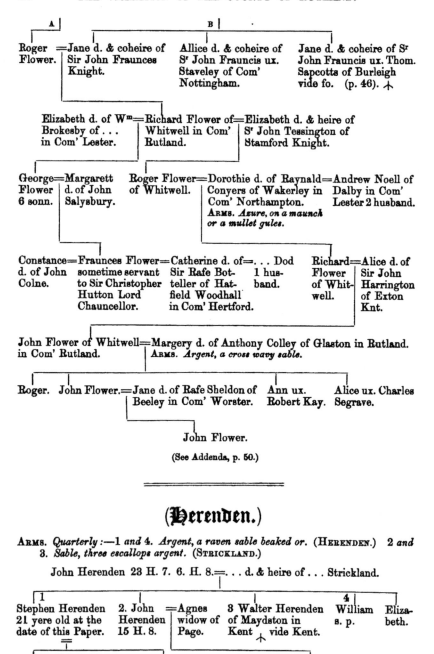

A |

Roger =Jane d. & coheire of
Flower. | Sir John Fraunces
| Knight.

B |

Allice d. & coheire of
Sᵣ John Frauncis ux.
Staveley of Com'
Nottingham.

Jane d. & coheire of Sᵣ
John Frauncis ux. Thom.
Sapcotts of Burleigh
vide fo. (p. 46).

Elizabeth d. of Wᵐ=Richard Flower of=Elizabeth d. & heire of
Brokesby of . . . | Whitwell in Com' | Sᵣ John Tessington of
in Com' Lester. | Rutland. | Stamford Knight.

George=Margarett
Flower | d. of John
6 sonn. | Salysbury.

Roger Flower=Dorothie d. of Raynald=Andrew Noell of
of Whitwell. | Conyers of Wakerley in | Dalby in Com'
| Com' Northampton. | Lester 2 husband.
| ARMS. *Azure, on a maunch*
| *or a mullet gules.*

Constance=Fraunces Flower=Catherine d. of=. . . Dod
d. of John | sometime servant | Sir Rafe Bot- | 1 hus-
Colne. | to Sir Christopher | teller of Hat- | band.
| Hutton Lord | field Woodhall
| Chauncellor. | in Com' Hertford.

Richard=Alice d. of
Flower | Sir John
of Whit- | Harrington
well. | of Exton
| Knt.

John Flower of Whitwell=Margery d. of Anthony Colley of Glaston in Rutland.
in Com' Rutland. | ARMS. *Argent, a cross wavy sable.*

Roger.   John Flower.=Jane d. of Rafe Sheldon of   Ann ux.   Alice ux. Charles
| Beeley in Com' Worster.   Robert Kay.   Segrave.

John Flower.

(See Addenda, p. 50.)

(Herenden.)

ARMS. *Quarterly :—1 and 4. Argent, a raven sable beaked or.* (HERENDEN.) *2 and
3. Sable, three escallops argent.* (STRICKLAND.)

John Herenden 23 H. 7. 6. H. 8.=. . . d. & heire of . . . Strickland.

1
Stephen Herenden
21 yere old at the
date of this Paper.

2. John =Agnes
Herenden | widow of
15 H. 8. | Page.

3 Walter Herenden
of Maydston in
Kent   vide Kent.

4
William   Eliza-
s. p.   beth.

Edward Herenden
of London.

2. Hen. Hereden of . . .
in Com' Rutland.

Ellenor d. & heire ux.
Edmond Page of Thorne.

Calcott.

ARMS. *Quarterly of six:*—1. *Argent, three bends sable.* CALCOTT. 2.   , *a chevron*   . 3. *Argent, on a bend gules three bulls' heads cabossed of the field.* 4. *Argent, fretty and a canton sable.* 5. *Azure, a fleur-de-lis argent.* 6. *Per pale gules and sable, a lion rampant argent.*

Noate y[t] I saw these coates as they are quartered since I wrote a coppy of this dissent and over them was written Caldecott of Ketton but whether this be true or no q'ry.

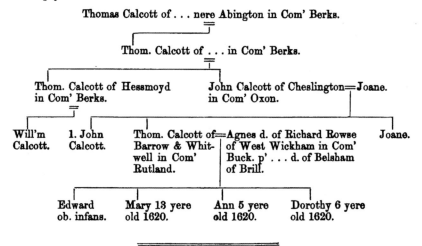

Thomas Calcott of . . . nere Abington in Com' Berks.

Thom. Calcott of . . . in Com' Berks.

Thom. Calcott of Hessmoyd in Com' Berks.

John Calcott of Cheslington=Joane. in Com' Oxon.

Will'm Calcott.

1. John Calcott.

Thom. Calcott of=Agnes d. of Richard Rowse Barrow & Whit-well in Com' Rutland.

of West Wickham in Com' Buck. p' . . . d. of Belsham of Brill.

Joane.

Edward ob. infans.

Mary 13 yere old 1620.

Ann 5 yere old 1620.

Dorothy 6 yere old 1620.

Berie.

ARMS. *Quarterly :*—1 and 4. *Ermine, on a bend engrailed or between two cotises gules three fleurs-de-lis azure.* (BERIE.) 2. *Ermine, a lion rampant azure, crowned or, charged on the breast with a crescent or.* (PICKERING.) 3. *Argent, three chaplets gules.* (LASSELLS.)

CREST. *A demi-wyvern argent, wings and feet sable, purfled or.*

This coate & Crest was past by Clarenceux Harvey 1565.

William Berie of Ashwell in Com' Rut-=Edith d. & heire of James Pickering of land who came out of the house of Berie | Tichmarsh in Com' Northampton 2. sonn of Collyton in Com' Devon. | of Gilbert Pickering of Titchmarsh.

Jane d. of=Gilbert Bery of Eayton==Rose d. of   William=. . . d. of . . .   Robert John   in Com' Lester m. to his   Francis   Berie of   Dryden of   Berie Smyth of   3 wife Alison d. of Hugh   Sherrard   Ashby in   of Withcock   Dennis of Pulchere   of Staple-   Com' North-   Grant-1 wife.   church in Com' Gloster   ford in Com'   ampton.   ham in of whome there is issue.   Lester 2   Com' as in Lester (p. 207).   wife.   Lin-con.

木   ▲   B

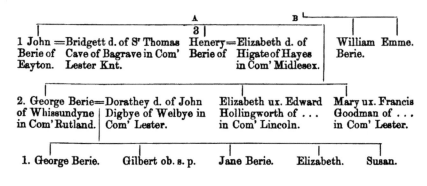

A   B

1 John =Bridgett d. of Sʳ Thomas   Henery=Elizabeth d. of   William   Emme.
Berie of Cave of Bagrave in Com'   Berie of Higate of Hayes   Berie.
Eayton.   Lester Knt.   in Com' Midlesex.

2. George Berie=Dorathey d. of John   Elizabeth ux. Edward   Mary ux. Francis
of Whissundyne | Digbye of Welbye in   Hollingworth of ...   Goodman of ...
in Com' Rutland. | Com' Lester.   in Com' Lincoln.   in Com' Lester.

1. George Berie.   Gilbert ob. s. p.   Jane Berie.   Elizabeth.   Susan.

(Wingfeld.)

ARMS. *Quarterly of twelve :*—1. *Argent, on a bend gules three vols of the field.*
(WINGFELD.) 2. *Argent, nine torteaux.* (HONEYPOT.) 3. *Quarterly, sable
and or.* (BOVILE.) 4. *Gules, a cross argent within a bordure engrailed or.**
(CARBONEL.) 5. *Gules, a lion rampant or.* (FITZALAN.) 6. *Azure, a wolf's
head erased argent.* (LUPUS.) 7. *Azure, three garbs or.* (BLUNDEVILL.)
8.   , *semée de lis   , within a bordure   charged with ten lions
passant   . 9. Chequy or and azure.* (WARREN.) 10. *Gules, a bend
fusilly or.* 11. *Argent, on a chief azure three crosses fitchées of the field.*
12. *Sable, three garbs argent.   Over all a crescent for difference.*

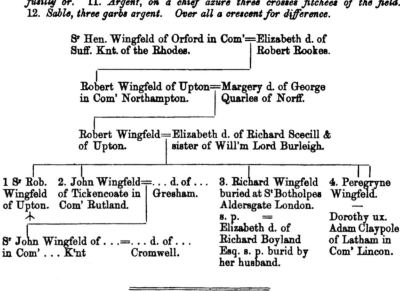

Sʳ Hen. Wingfeld of Orford in Com'=Elizabeth d. of
Suff. Knt. of the Rhodes.   Robert Rookes.

Robert Wingfeld of Upton=Margery d. of George
in Com' Northampton.   Quarles of Norff.

Robert Wingfeld=Elizabeth d. of Richard Scecill &
of Upton.   sister of Will'm Lord Burleigh.

1 Sʳ Rob.   2. John Wingfeld=... d. of ...   3. Richard Wingfeld   4. Peregryne
Wingfeld   of Tickencoate in | Gresham.   buried at Sᵗ Botholpes Wingfeld.
of Upton.   Com' Rutland.   Aldersgate London.   —
                                                s. p.   =   Dorothy ux.
Sʳ John Wingfeld of ...=... d. of ...   Elizabeth d. of   Adam Claypole
in Com' ... K'nt   Cromwell.   Richard Boyland   of Latham in
                                                Esq. s. p. burid by   Com' Lincon.
                                                her husband.

* This is the Coat of Carbonel, which was brought into the family by the marriage of Sir Thomas
Wingfeld with Margaret, *wilow* of Wm. Carbonell and *d. and h.* of William Bovile, *ante,* 1378.

(Catesby.)

ARMS. *Argent, two lions passant guardant sable, crowned or.*   *Visit. Northampton.*
CREST. *A leopard passant guardant argent pellettée.*   *Harl. MS.* 1094, *fo.* 93.)

Sr John Catesby Knt. Justice=Elizabeth d. of Walter Greene of Bridgnorth.
of the Common bench. | ARMS. *Azure, a chevron between three bucks or.*

Sr Humfrey Catesby a quo   Francis.   Euseby Catesby=Anne d. & heire of John
Catesby de Whiston in   of Seaton in   Seaton of Seaton in
Com' Northampton.   Com' Rutland.   Com' Rutland.

Edward Catesby of Seaton.=Anne d. of Thomas Haselrigge.

Michell Catesby of Seaton.=Ann d. of James or John Odim or Obbone.

1 Richard Catesby=...d. of ...   2. Erasmus=...d. & heire of ...
of Seaton.   Harrison.   Catesby.   Woodhall de Kenelworth.

Edward Catesby.   Michell Catesby.

3. Kenelme Catesby=Alice d. of Judkin vel Rudkin of   Wibora ux. Richard
of Seaton.   Preston in Com' Rutland.   Weston, Justice of
the Common bench.

Michell Catesby.

(Brisko.)

(ARMS. *Argent, three greyhounds courant in pale sable.*
CREST. *A greyhound courant sable seizing a hare or.*   *Harl MS.* 1504, *fo.* 63.)

Robert Brisko of Crofton in Com' Comb'land.=

Edward Brisko of West Ward in Comb'land younger Sonn.=

2. Edward Brisko of=Catherin d.   1. Guy Brisko   3 Thomas=...d. of ...
Aldenham in Com'   of ...   of West   Brisko   Huddard sister
Hertford.   Huddard.   Ward.   ob. s. p.   of Catherin.

A

F

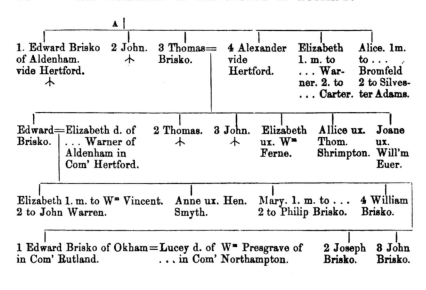

A

1. Edward Brisko of Aldenham. vide Hertford.

2 John.

3 Thomas = Brisko.

4 Alexander vide Hertford.

Elizabeth 1. m. to ... Warner. 2. to ... Carter.

Alice. 1m. to ... Bromfeld 2 to Silvester Adams.

Edward = Elizabeth d. of Brisko. | ... Warner of Aldenham in Com' Hertford.

2 Thomas.

3 John.

Elizabeth ux. Wm Ferne.

Allice ux. Thom. Shrimpton.

Joane ux. Will'm Euer.

Elizabeth 1. m. to Wm Vincent. 2 to John Warren.

Anne ux. Hen. Smyth.

Mary. 1. m. to ... 2 to Philip Brisko.

4 William Brisko.

1 Edward Brisko of Okham = Lucey d. of Wm Presgrave of in Com' Rutland.   ... in Com' Northampton.

2 Joseph Brisko.

3 John Brisko.

(Roberts.)

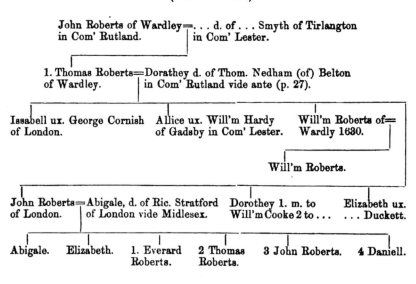

John Roberts of Wardley = ... d. of ... Smyth of Tirlangton in Com' Rutland. | in Com' Lester.

1. Thomas Roberts = Dorathey d. of Thom. Nedham (of) Belton of Wardley. | in Com' Rutland vide ante (p. 27).

Issabell ux. George Cornish of London.

Allice ux. Will'm Hardy of Gadsby in Com' Lester.

Will'm Roberts of = Wardly 1630.

Will'm Roberts.

John Roberts = Abigale, d. of Ric. Stratford of London. | of London vide Midlesex.

Dorothey 1. m. to Will'm Cooke 2 to ...

Elizabeth ux. ... Duckett.

Abigale.

Elizabeth.

1. Everard Roberts.

2 Thomas Roberts.

3 John Roberts.

4 Daniell.

(Tooke.)

ARMS. *Quarterly :—1 and 4. Gules, three T's argent within a bordure vairé argent and sable.* (TOOKY.) *2. Quarterly argent and gules, a bend sable.* (MANEWARD.) *3. Argent, a fess gules surmounted by a bend sable.* (LITHAM OF REDBORNE.)

CREST. *A demi-seahorse rampant quarterly gules and or, ducally gorged per pale or and gules.*

Noah Tooky of South Luffenham in Com' Rutland. =

Berefford.

ARMS. *Argent, on a chevron azure three crosses pattée or.*

Bodendyne of Bellinerthorpe.

ARMS. *Quarterly :—1. Azure, a fess between three chess-rooks or. 2. Barry of six or and sable.*

Tissington.

ARMS. *Quarterly :—1.   on a bend three roundels (untinctured). 2. Argent, a chevron sable between three fleurs-de-lis vert.*

Warren.

ARMS. *Quarterly, argent and sable, four foxes' heads couped, counterchanged, collared gules.*

Hutton of Glaston.

ARMS. *Quarterly :—1. Vert, an eagle displayed or. 2.   a cross humettée flory between four escallops.*

Plessington of Burley.

ARMS. *Quarterly :—1. Azure, a cross flory between four martlets argent. 2. Or, a lion rampant azure, surmounted by a bend compony argent and gules.*

Harington of Glaston.

ARMS. *Quarterly:*—1. *Or, a chief azure, over all a bend engrailed gules.* 2. *Gules, a griffin segreant argent.* 3. *Barry of ten argent and gules, a canton of the last.*

Popley of Keton.

ARMS. *Quarterly:*—1. *Argent, a bend sable.* 2.   *three crosses flory*

Cheny of Seaton.

ARMS. *Quarterly:*—1. *Chequy argent and azure, a fess gules fretty or.* 2. *Argent, a lion rampant gules.*

Palmes.

ARMS. *Quarterly:*—1. *Gules, three fleurs-de-lis argent, a chief vair, a crescent for difference.* 2. *Or, two chevrons between three martlets sable.* 3. *Argent, on a chief sable three griffins' heads erased of the field.*

Barkly.

ARMS. *Quarterly:*—1. *Gules, a chevron between ten cinquefoils argent.* 2. *Azure, a lion rampant guardant argent, crowned or.*

Bassett of North Luffenham.

ARMS. *Quarterly:*—1. *Or, three piles meeting in base gules; on a canton argent thee bars wavy azure.* 2. *Argent, two bars, and in chief three cinquefoils gules.*

Cabe of Baroughbon.

ARMS. *Quarterly of six :*—1. *Azure, fretty argent.* (CAVE.) 2. *Ermine, on a chevron sable three brocks' heads erased argent.* (GEVILL.) 3. *Argent, a chevron between three popinjays vert, membered gules.* (CLIFFE.) 4. *Sable, a cross flory ermine.* 5. *Argent, a fess sable between three cocks gules.*

Ogle.

ARMS. *Quarterly :*—1. *Or, a fess between three crescents, each including a fleur-de-lis gules.* 2. *Or, an orle azure.*

Belgrabe.

ARMS. *Quarterly*—1. *Gules, a chevron ermine between three mascles voided argent.* 2. *Ermine, three mascles conjoined in fess, voided gules.*

Thomas Sapcotts of Burleigh.

ARMS. *Quarterly :*—1. *Sable, three dovecotes argent.* (SAPCOTTS.) 2. *Gules, four fusils conjoined in fess.* (DENHAM.) 3. *Gules, three bezants, a label of three points azure.* (HYDON.) 4. *Gules, three door-arches argent, their capitals and pedestals or, those in chief single, that in base double.* (ARCHES.)

Henery Conney of Parley.

p' C. Camden 1609.

ARMS. *Argent, a saltire gules between four conies sejant sable.*
CREST. *On a mount vert a cony sejant or.*

Webster.

ARMS. *Or, a chevron engrailed gules, in chief two torteaux, in base a cross pattée of the second.*

Harington.

ARMS. *Quarterly of twenty-four :*—1. *Sable, a fret argent.* (HARINGTON.) 2. *Argent, three bars gules.* (MULTON.) 3. *Azure, semée-de-lis fretty or.* (MORVILL.) 4. *Argent, a chevron between three billets gules.* (DE LA LAUNDE.) 5. *Argent, a bend engrailed gules.* (COLEPEPER.) 6. *(Argent), a chevron (sable) between ten martlets (gules).* (HARDRESHULL.) 7. *(Or), a cross engrailed (gules), in the dexter chief a martlet (vert).* (HAWTE.) 8. *Azure, three stags statant or.* (GREENE.) 9. *Argent, fretty sable; on a canton of the last a mullet or.* (IWARDBY.) 10. *Azure, a saltire and a chief or.* (BRUSE.) 11. *Argent, an escocheon within a double tressure flory counterflory gules.* (ANGUISH.) 12. *Argent, a lion rampant azure, a chief gules.* (WALTHERS.) 13. *(Azure), three garbs (or).* (CHESTER.) 14. *Azure, a wolf's head erased argent.* (LUPUS.) 15. *Azure, a cinquefoil argent.* (MOTON.) 16. *Or, three piles meeting in base gules, a canton vair.* (BASSET.) 17. *Or, a fess gules.* (AVENEL.) 18. *Ermine, a bend gules.* (ELMSTED ?) 19. *Sable, three dovecotes argent.* (SAPCOTTS.) 20. *Gules, four fusils conjoined in fess ermine.* (DENHAM.)

" After Denham must come 4 Coates more as on the leaffe affore " (viz)

21. *Gules, three bezants, a label of three points azure.* (HYDON.) 22. *Gules, three door-arches argent, their capitals and pedestals or, those in chief single, that in base double.* (ARCHES.) 23. *Argent, a chevron between three eagles displayed gules.* (FRANCES.) 24. *Azure, a cross patonce between four martlets argent.* (PLESSINGTON.) *Over all, on an escocheon of pretence, a baronet's hand gules.*

" The quartered Coates for the Baronetts Family must bee as they are on the leaffe affore " (viz, the twenty four quarterings).

" Sᵣ James Harington the last Baronett must quarter 6 Coates more as in Oxford-shire vide Oxon."*

CREST. *A lion's head erased or, gorged with a belt gules, buckled of the first.*

(Harington.)

Sᵣ John Harington of Exton = Elizabeth d. & heire of Robert Moton
in Com' Rutland Knt. | of Peckleton in com' Lester.

Sᵣ James Harington = Lucey sister of Sir   2 Edward.   3 Robert.   4 John
of Exton Knt. | Henery Sidney Knt. | | | Hastings (?).

Ellinor ux. Sᵣ Edward Mountacute of Boughton in Com' Northampton.	Frances ux. Sᵣ Wᵐ Leigh of Newnham in Com' Warwick.	Mary ux. Sᵣ Edward Wingfeld of Kymbalton in Com' Huntington Knt.	Theodosia ux. Edward Sutton Lord Dudley.
Margeret ux. Bennett Sisano. Castiliano.	Catherin ux. Sᵣ Edward Dymoke of . . . in Com' . . . Knt.	Mabell ux. Sᵣ Andrew Noell of Dalby in Com' Lester.	Susan 1 m. to Francis Lord Hastings. 2. to Sᵣ George Kingsmill 3. to Edward Lord Zouch.

* 25. *Or, two bends azure.* (DOYLEY.) 26. *Argent, a cock sable, beaked and wattled gules.* (MOORE.) 27. *Sable, a lion rampant guardant or.* (BROCAS.) 28. *Sable, two lions passant guardant argent.* (ROGERS) 29. *Argent, a cross between four mullets of six points gules.* (BANBURY.) 30. *Argent, on a bend gules three fleurs-de-lis or.* (COULSON.)

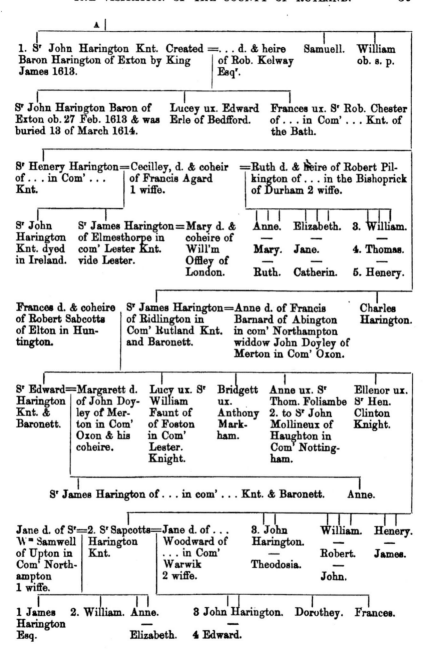

A

1. Sʳ John Harington Knt. Created ═ . . . d. & heire   Samuell.   William
Baron Harington of Exton by King │ of Rob. Kelway   ob. s. p.
James 1613. │ Esqʳ.

Sʳ John Harington Baron of   Lucey ux. Edward   Frances ux. Sʳ Rob. Chester
Exton ob. 27 Feb. 1613 & was   Erle of Bedfford.   of . . . in Com' . . . Knt. of
buried 13 of March 1614. the Bath.

Sʳ Henery Harington═Cecilley, d. & coheir   ═Ruth d. & heire of Robert Pil-
of . . . in Com' . . . │ of Francis Agard   kington of . . . in the Bishoprick
Knt. │ 1 wiffe.   of Durham 2 wiffe.

Sʳ John   Sʳ James Harington═Mary d. &   Anne.   Elizabeth.   3. William.
Harington   of Elmesthorpe in │ coheire of   —   —   —
Knt. dyed   com' Lester Knt.   Will'm   Mary.   Jane.   4. Thomas.
in Ireland.   vide Lester.   Offley of   —   —   —
London.   Ruth.   Catherin.   5. Henery.

Frances d. & coheire   Sʳ James Harington═Anne d. of Francis   Charles
of Robert Sabcotts   of Ridlington in   Barnard of Abington   Harington.
of Elton in Hun-   Com' Rutland Knt.   in com' Northampton
tington.   and Baronett.   widdow John Doyley of
Merton in Com' Oxon.

Sʳ Edward═Margarett d.   Lucy ux. Sʳ   Bridgett   Anne ux. Sʳ   Ellenor ux.
Harington │ of John Doy-   William   ux.   Thom. Foliambe   Sʳ Hen.
Knt. & │ ley of Mer-   Faunt of   Anthony   2. to Sʳ John   Clinton
Baronett. │ ton in Com'   of Foston   Mark-   Mollineux of   Knight.
Oxon & his   in Com'   ham.   Haughton in
coheire.   Lester.   Com' Notting-
Knight.   ham.

Sʳ James Harington of . . . in com' . . . Knt. & Baronett.   Anne.

Jane d. of Sʳ═2. Sʳ Sapcotts═Jane d. of . . .   3. John   William.   Henery.
Wᵐ Samwell │ Harington │ Woodward of   Harington.   —   —
of Upton in │ Knt. │ . . . in Com'   —   Robert.   James.
Com' North- │ │ Warwik   Theodosia.   —
ampton   2 wiffe.   John.
1 wiffe.

1 James   2. William.   Anne.   3 John Harington.   Dorothey.   Frances.
Harington   —
Esq.   Elizabeth.   4 Edward.

(Durant.)

Arms. *Quarterly:*—1. *Sable, a cross crosslet ermine.* (Durant.) 2. *Argent, two bars, and in chief three fleurs-de-lis gules.* (S^r. Lise.*) 3. *Sable, a fess dancettée and in chief three fleurs-de-lis argent.* 4. *Gules, a chevron between three lions' gambs erased ermine.*

Crest. *A boar passant argent, bristled or, vulned over the left shoulder gules.*

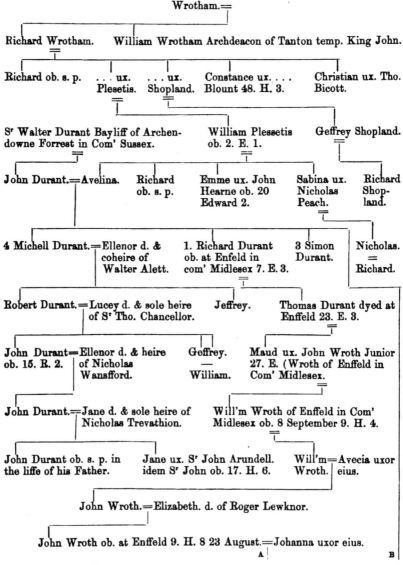

Wrotham.=

Richard Wrotham. William Wrotham Archdeacon of Tanton temp. King John.

Richard ob. s. p. . . . ux. Plesetis. . . . ux. Shopland. Constance ux. . . . Blount 48. H. 3. Christian ux. Tho. Bicott.

Sr Walter Durant Bayliff of Archendowne Forrest in Com' Sussex. William Plessetis ob. 2. E. 1. Geffrey Shopland.

John Durant.=Avelina. Richard ob. s. p. Emme ux. John Hearne ob. 20 Edward 2. Sabina ux. Nicholas Peach. Richard Shopland.

4 Michell Durant.=Ellenor d. & coheire of Walter Alett. 1. Richard Durant ob. at Enfeld in com' Midlesex 7. E. 3. 3 Simon Durant. Nicholas. = Richard.

Robert Durant.=Lucey d. & sole heire of Sr Tho. Chancellor. Jeffrey. Thomas Durant dyed at Enffeld 23. E. 3.

John Durant=Ellenor d. & heire ob. 15. R. 2. of Nicholas Wansfford. Geffrey. — William. Maud ux. John Wroth Junior 27. E. (Wroth of Enffeld in Com' Midlesex.

John Durant.=Jane d. & sole heire of Nicholas Trevathion. Will'm Wroth of Enffeld in Com' Midlesex ob. 8 September 9. H. 4.

John Durant ob. s. p. in the liffe of his Father. Jane ux. Sr John Arundell. idem Sr John ob. 17. H. 6. Will'm Wroth.=Avecia uxor eius.

John Wroth.=Elizabeth. d. of Roger Lewknor.

John Wroth ob. at Enffeld 9. H. 8 23 August.=Johanna uxor eius.

A B

* This coat for St Lisle is impaled with Durant in Camden's grants, July, 1606.

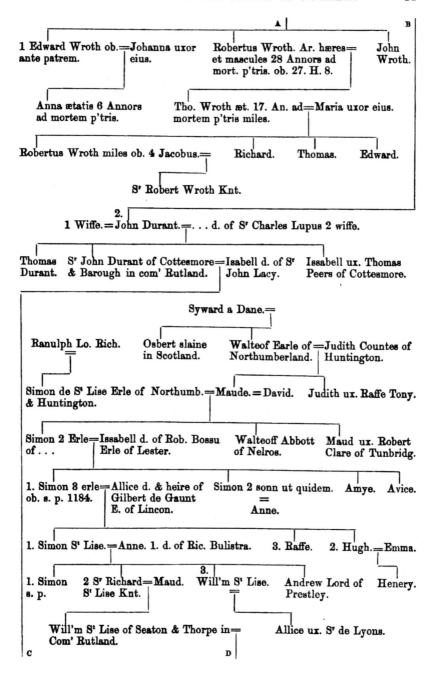

A | B

1 Edward Wroth ob.=Johanna uxor | Robertus Wroth. Ar. hæres= | John
ante patrem. | eius. | et mascules 28 Annors ad | Wroth.
| | mort. p'tris. ob. 27. H. 8. |

Anna ætatis 6 Annors | Tho. Wroth æt. 17. An. ad=Maria uxor eius.
ad mortem p'tris. | mortem p'tris miles.

Robertus Wroth miles ob. 4 Jacobus.= | Richard. | Thomas. | Edward.

Sr Robert Wroth Knt.

2.
1 Wiffe.=John Durant.=. . . d. of Sr Charles Lupus 2 wiffe.

Thomas | Sr John Durant of Cottesmore=Isabell d. of Sr | Issabell ux. Thomas
Durant. | & Barough in com' Rutland. | John Lacy. | Peers of Cottesmore.

Syward a Dane.=

Ranulph Lo. Rich. | Osbert slaine | Walteof Earle of=Judith Countes of
= | in Scotland. | Northumberland. | Huntington.

Simon de St Lise Erle of Northumb.=Maude.=David. | Judith ux. Raffe Tony.
& Huntington.

Simon 2 Erle=Issabell d. of Rob. Bossu | Walteoff Abbott | Maud ux. Robert
of . . . | Erle of Lester. | of Nelros. | Clare of Tunbridg.

1. Simon 3 erle=Allice d. & heire of | Simon 2 sonn ut quidem. | Amye. | Avice.
ob. s. p. 1184. | Gilbert de Gaunt | =
| E. of Lincon. | Anne.

1. Simon St Lise.=Anne. 1. d. of Ric. Bulistra. | 3. Raffe. | 2. Hugh.=Emma.

3.
1. Simon | 2 Sr Richard=Maud. | Will'm St Lise. | Andrew Lord of | Henery.
s. p. | St Lise Knt. | = | Prestley.

Will'm St Lise of Seaton & Thorpe in= | Allice ux. Sr de Lyons.
Com' Rutland.

C | D

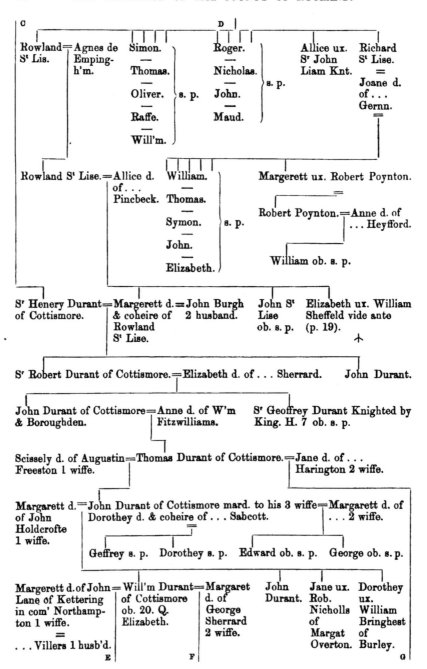

C

D

Rowland=Agnes de   Simon.   Roger.   Allice ux.   Richard
S' Lis. Emping-   —   —   S' John   S' Lise.
         h'm.   Thomas.   Nicholas.   Liam Knt.   =
                    —   —   s. p.   Joane d.
                    Oliver. s. p. John.   of . . .
                    —   —   Gernn.
                    Raffe.   Maud.   =
                    —
                    Will'm.

Rowland S' Lise.=Allice d.   William.   Margerett ux. Robert Poynton.
                 of . . .   —   =
                 Pincbeck.   Thomas.   Robert Poynton.=Anne d. of
                              —   . . . Heyfford.
                              Symon. s. p.
                              —   William ob. s. p.
                              John.
                              —
                              Elizabeth.

S' Henery Durant=Margerett d.=John Burgh   John S'   Elizabeth ux. William
of Cottismore.   & coheire of 2 husband.   Lise   Sheffeld vide ante
                 Rowland   ob. s. p. (p. 19).
                 S' Lise.

S' Robert Durant of Cottismore.=Elizabeth d. of . . . Sherrard.   John Durant.

John Durant of Cottismore=Anne d. of W'm   S' Geoffrey Durant Knighted by
& Boroughden.   Fitzwilliams.   King. H. 7 ob. s. p.

Scissely d. of Augustin=Thomas Durant of Cottismore.=Jane d. of . . .
Freeston 1 wiffe.   Harington 2 wiffe.

Margarett d.=John Durant of Cottismore mard. to his 3 wiffe=Margarett d. of
of John | Dorothey d. & coheire of . . . Sabcott. | . . . 2 wiffe.
Holdcrofte | |
1 wiffe. | = |
          Geffrey s. p.   Dorothey s. p.   Edward ob. s. p.   George ob. s. p.

Margerett d. of John= Will'm Durant=Margaret   John   Jane ux.   Dorothey
Lane of Kettering   of Cottismore d. of   Durant.   Rob.   ux.
in com' Northamp-   ob. 20. Q.   George   Nicholls   William
ton 1 wiffe.   Elizabeth.   Sherrard   of   Bringhest
=   2 wiffe.   Margat   of
. . . Villers 1 husb'd.   Overton.   Burley.

E   F   G

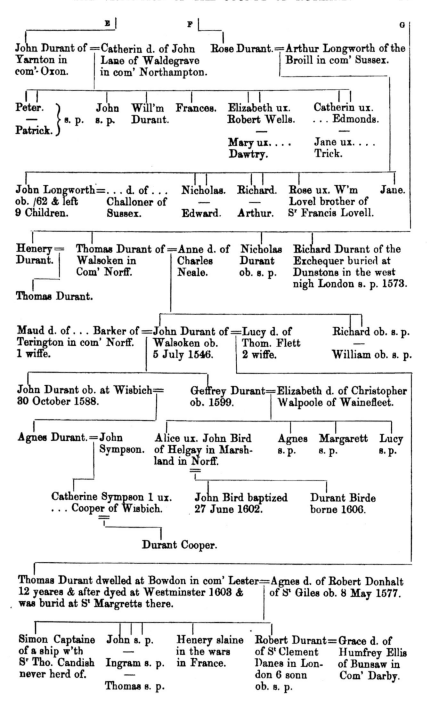

E | F | G |

John Durant of =Catherin d. of John   Rose Durant.=Arthur Longworth of the
Yarnton in   Lane of Waldegrave   Broill in com' Sussex.
com'- Oxon.   in com' Northampton.

Peter.   John   Will'm   Frances.   Elizabeth ux.   Catherin ux.
—   } s. p. s. p. Durant.   Robert Wells.   ... Edmonds.
Patrick.)

                                             Mary ux. ...   Jane ux. ...
                                             Dawtry.   Trick.

John Longworth=... d. of ...   Nicholas.   Richard.   Rose ux. W'm   Jane.
ob. /62 & left   Challoner of   —   —   Lovel brother of
9 Children.   Sussex.   Edward.   Arthur.   Sr Francis Lovell.

Henery =   Thomas Durant of =Anne d. of   Nicholas   Richard Durant of the
Durant.   Walsoken in   Charles   Durant   Exchequer buried at
            Com' Norff.   Neale.   ob. s. p. Dunstons in the west
                                                      nigh London s. p. 1573.
Thomas Durant.

Maud d. of ... Barker of =John Durant of =Lucy d. of   Richard ob. s. p.
Terington in com' Norff. Walsoken ob.   Thom. Flett   —
1 wiffe.   5 July 1546.   2 wiffe.   William ob. s. p.

John Durant ob. at Wisbich=   Geffrey Durant=Elizabeth d. of Christopher
30 October 1588.   ob. 1599.   Walpoole of Wainefleet.

Agnes Durant.=John   Alice ux. John Bird   Agnes   Margarett   Lucy
             Sympson.   of Helgay in Marsh-   s. p.   s. p.   s. p.
                        land in Norff.

       Catherine Sympson 1 ux.   John Bird baptized   Durant Birde
       ... Cooper of Wisbich.   27 June 1602.   borne 1606.

                   Durant Cooper.

Thomas Durant dwelled at Bowdon in com' Lester=Agnes d. of Robert Donhalt
12 yeares & after dyed at Westminster 1603 &   of St Giles ob. 8 May 1577.
was burid at St Margretts there.

Simon Captaine   John s. p.   Henery slaine   Robert Durant=Grace d. of
of a ship w'th   —   in the wars   of St Clement Humfrey Ellis
Sr Tho. Candish Ingram s. p. in France.   Danes in Lon- of Bunsaw in
never herd of.   don 6 sonn   Com' Darby.
                 Thomas s. p.   ob. s. p.

(𝔖ympson.)

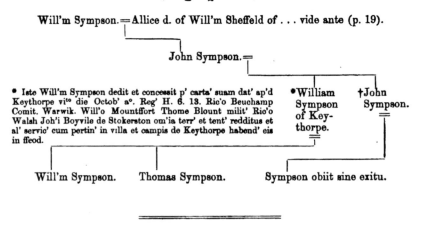

Will'm Sympson.=Allice d. of Will'm Sheffeld of . . . vide ante (p. 19).

John Sympson.=

* Iste Will'm Sympson dedit et concessit p' carta' suam dat' ap'd Keythorpe vi⁰ die Octob' a°. Reg' H. 6. 13. Ric'o Beuchamp Comit. Warwik. Will'o Mountffort Thome Blount milit' Ric'o Walsh Joh'i Boyvile de Stokerston om'ia terr' et tent' redditus et al' servio' cum pertin' in villa et campis de Keythorpe habend' eis in ffeod.

*William Sympson of Keythorpe.

†John Sympson.=

Will'm Sympson.   Thomas Sympson.   Sympson obiit sine exitu.

(ℌaselwood.)

Arms. *Quarterly of six :—1. Argent, a chevron between three hazel leaves vert.* (Haselwood). *2. Sable, a chevron ermine between three owls argent, on a chief three hazel branches*   (.) *3.   , a chevron between three squirrels séjant gules.* (.) *4. Or, on a chevron azure, between three fleurs-de-lis sable, as many bars gemelles*   (   ). *5.   , a chevron between two trefoils in chief and a fleur-de-lis in base sable.* (   ).

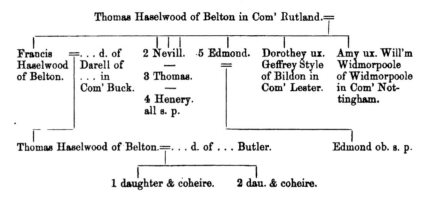

Thomas Haselwood of Belton in Com' Rutland.=

Francis Haselwood of Belton. =. . . d. of Darell of . . . in Com' Buck.

2 Nevill.
—
3 Thomas.
—
4 Henery.
all s. p.

5 Edmond.
=

Dorothey ux. Geffrey Style of Bildon in Com' Lester.

Amy ux. Will'm Widmorpoole of Widmorpoole in Com' Nottingham.

Thomas Haselwood of Belton.=. . . d. of . . . Butler.   Edmond ob. s. p.

1 daughter & coheire.   2 dau. & coheire.

---

† Iste Joh'es p' Cart' sua' dat' 8 die Octob. 8 Reg' H. 6. 13 relaxavit preffat' Cart' et aliis ter' et ten' in Keythorpe que habuen' ex . . . dono Will'mi Sympson fratris sui.

(Andrewes.)

ARMS. *Quarterly of six* :—1. *Gules, on a saltire or another vert.* (ANDREWS.) 2. *Azure, fretty argent.* (CAVE.) 3. *Ermine, on a chevron sable three brocs' heads erased argent.* (GEVILL.) 4. *Argent, a chevron between three popingays vert.* (CLIFFE.) 5. *Or, a lion rampant crowned gules.* (.) 6. *Or, chevron sable within a bordure engrailed gules.* (.)

Anthony Andrewes of Pisbrooke.=

(Allington.)

ARMS. *Quarterly of six* :—1. *Sable, a bend engrailed between six billets argent.* (   ). 2. *Gules, on a bend argent three leopards' heads sable.* (.) 3. *Gules, three covered cups argent.* (.) 4.   , *ten martlets*   , *a canton*   . (.) 5. *Per fess*   *and*   , *a pale counterchanged on the first, three griffins' heads erased*   . (   ).

Hugho Allington of Timwell in Com' Rutland.

(Fielding of Mastrop.)

ARMS. *Quarterly of nine* :—1. *Argent, on a fess azure three lozenges or.* (FIELDING.) 2. *Ermine, on a fess vert three escallops or.* (NAPTON.) 3. *(Azure), three stirrups (or).* (PURIFOY.) 4.   , *a leopard's face between a chief and a chevron*   . (.) 5. *Per pale gules and sable, a lion rampant argent.* (BOLLERS.) 6. *Gules, a bend argent between six martlets (argent).* (SEYTON.) 7. *Argent, on a chevron sable three escallops or, in chief a fox courant*   , *within a bordure engrailed*   . (.) 8. *(Argent), a fess dancettée gules, in chief three leopards' faces sable.* (POUTNEY.) 9. *Gules, a saltire vair.* (WILLINGTON.)

(Dive of Ridlington.)

(Sherrard of Whitsondyne.)

ARMS. *Quarterly of six* :—1. *Argent, a chevron gules between three torteaux.* (SHERRARD.) 2. *Argent, on a bend sable nine annulets interlaced in threes or.* (HAUBURKE or HUBARD.) 3. *Ermine, on a chevron sable three bezants within a bordure engrailed gules.* (HELWELL.) 4. *Gules, on a chevron argent three roses of the field.* (BROW.) 5. *(Argent), a fess and canton conjoined gules within a bordure sable bezantée.* (WOODVILE.)

(𝕾apcotts.)

ARMS. *See ante, p.* 37.

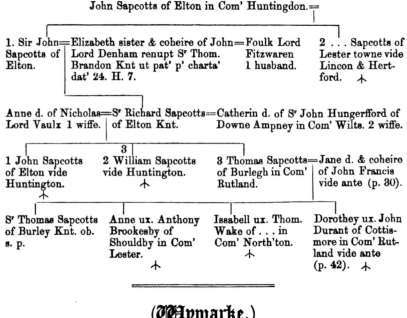

John Sapcotts of Elton in Com' Huntingdon.═

1. Sir John═Elizabeth sister & coheire of John═Foulk Lord   2 ... Sapcotts of
Sapcotts of │ Lord Denham renupt Sʳ Thom.   Fitzwaren   Lester towne vide
Elton.   │ Brandon Knt ut pat' p' charta' 1 husband.   Lincon & Hert-
            │ dat' 24. H. 7.   ford.

Anne d. of Nicholas═Sʳ Richard Sapcotts═Catherin d. of Sʳ John Hungerfford of
Lord Vaulx 1 wiffe. │ of Elton Knt.   Downe Ampney in Com' Wilts. 2 wiffe.

1 John Sapcotts   2 William Sapcotts   3 Thomas Sapcotts═Jane d. & coheire
of Elton vide   vide Huntington.   of Burlegh in Com'│ of John Francis
Huntington.   Rutland.   vide ante (p. 30).

Sʳ Thomas Sapcotts   Anne ux. Anthony   Issabell ux. Thom.   Dorothey ux. John
of Burley Knt. ob.   Brookesby of   Wake of ... in   Durant of Cottis-
s. p.   Shouldby in Com'   Com' North'ton.   more in Com' Rut-
                     Lester.   land vide ante
                                                                (p. 42).

(𝕬𝖞marke.)

ARMS. *Quarterly* :—1. *Argent, on a bend cotised azure the escocheons of the field.*
WYMARKE. 2. *Ermine, on a bend azure three cinquefoils or.* (BEWFFO.)

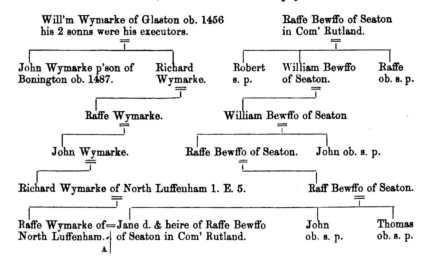

Will'm Wymarke of Glaston ob. 1456   Raffe Bewffo of Seaton
his 2 sonns were his executors.   in Com' Rutland.

John Wymarke p'son of   Richard   Robert   William Bewffo   Raffe
Bonington ob. 1487.   Wymarke.   s. p.   of Seaton.   ob. s. p.

        Raffe Wymarke.   William Bewffo of Seaton

        John Wymarke.   Raffe Bewffo of Seaton.   John ob. s. p.

Richard Wymarke of North Luffenham 1. E. 5.   Raff Bewffo of Seaton.

Raffe Wymarke of═Jane d. & heire of Raffe Bewffo   John   Thomas
North Luffenham. │ of Seaton in Com' Rutland.   ob. s. p.   ob. s. p.
        A

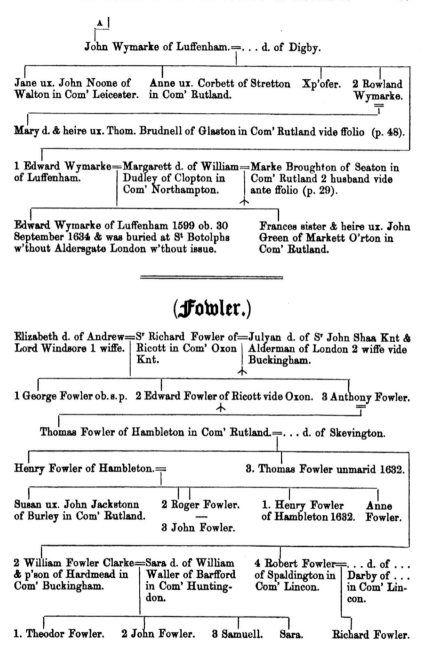

A |

John Wymarke of Luffenham.=... d. of Digby.

Jane ux. John Noone of Walton in Com' Leicester.   Anne ux. Corbett of Stretton in Com' Rutland.   Xp'ofer.   2 Rowland Wymarke. =

Mary d. & heire ux. Thom. Brudnell of Glaston in Com' Rutland vide ffolio (p. 48).

1 Edward Wymarke=Margarett d. of William=Marke Broughton of Seaton in
of Luffenham.   Dudley of Clopton in   Com' Rutland 2 husband vide
   Com' Northampton.   ante ffolio (p. 29).

Edward Wymarke of Luffenham 1599 ob. 30 September 1634 & was buried at St Botolphs w'thout Aldersgate London w'thout issue.   Frances sister & heire ux. John Green of Markett O'rton in Com' Rutland.

(Fowler.)

Elizabeth d. of Andrew=Sr Richard Fowler of=Julyan d. of Sr John Shaa Knt &
Lord Windsore 1 wiffe.   Ricott in Com' Oxon   Alderman of London 2 wiffe vide
   Knt.   Buckingham.

1 George Fowler ob. s. p.   2 Edward Fowler of Ricott vide Oxon.   3 Anthony Fowler. =

Thomas Fowler of Hambleton in Com' Rutland.=... d. of Skevington.

Henry Fowler of Hambleton.=   3. Thomas Fowler unmarid 1632.

Susan ux. John Jackstonn of Burley in Com' Rutland.   2 Roger Fowler. —   3 John Fowler.   1. Henry Fowler of Hambleton 1632.   Anne Fowler.

2 William Fowler Clarke=Sara d. of William
& p'son of Hardmead in   Waller of Barfford
Com' Buckingham.   in Com' Huntingdon.

4 Robert Fowler=... d. of ...
of Spaldington in   Darby of ...
Com' Lincon.   in Com' Lincon.

1. Theodor Fowler.   2 John Fowler.   8 Samuell.   Sara.   Richard Fowler.

(Brudnell.)

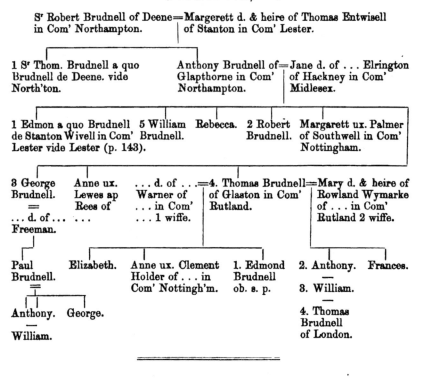

Sᵣ Robert Brudnell of Deene=Margerett d. & heire of Thomas Entwisell
in Com' Northampton. | of Stanton in Com' Lester.

1 Sᵣ Thom. Brudnell a quo   Anthony Brudnell of=Jane d. of . . . Elrington
Brudnell de Deene. vide   Glapthorne in Com' | of Hackney in Com'
North'ton.   Northampton. | Midlesex.

1 Edmon a quo Brudnell   5 William   Rebecca.   2 Robert   Margarett ux. Palmer
de Stanton Wivell in Com' Brudnell.   Brudnell. of Southwell in Com'
Lester vide Lester (p. 143).   Nottingham.

3 George   Anne ux.   . . . d. of . . .=4. Thomas Brudnell=Mary d. & heire of
Brudnell.   Lewes ap   Warner of | of Glaston in Com'   Rowland Wymarke
=   Rees of   . . . in Com' | Rutland.   of . . . in Com'
. . . d. of . . .   . 1 wiffe.   Rutland 2 wiffe.
Freeman.

Paul   Elizabeth.   Anne ux. Clement   1. Edmond   2. Anthony.   Frances.
Brudnell.   Holder of . . . in Brudnell   —
=   Com' Nottingh'm.   ob. s. p.   3. William.

Anthony.   George.   4. Thomas
—   Brudnell
William.   of London.

(Mackworth.)

Thomas de Normanvile ob. 8. H. 3.
=

Raphe de Normanvile ob. 43. H. 3.=Galiena.

1. Thomas de Normanvile ob. 11. E. 1.=Dionisia shee held her dower.   2 Raphe.

Margarett d. & heire 20 yeare old=Will'm de Basings ob. 9. E. 2
in aº. 33. E. 1. ob. 15. E. 3. | beffore his wiffe.

Thomas de Basings 16 yere old at the deth of his Father. ob. 23. E. 3. in Kent.
=

Sir John Basings Knt. ob. 7. R. 2.
=

A

A |

1. Sir John de Basings Knt. ob. 24. H. 6. s. p. what yeare
he was high Sheriff of Rutland. This S\[r] John had a base
sonn & a base daughter to whome he conveyed divers
lands in Com' Lincon & Rutland.

2. Thomas Basings
ob. 1. H. 4 s. p.
=
Agnes survived
her husband.

Mackworth of Mackworth.
=

Allice=Thomas Mack-
sister | worth Esq\[r] who
& | died before John
heire. | de Basings &
| his wiffe.

John Mackworth Deane of Lincolne gave certaine lands
in Darbye to Henery Mackworth sonn of Thomas Mack-
worth his brother as by a deed apereth dated at Mack-
worth 11. H. 6 & one other deed dated 24. H. 6. & sealed
with the Armes of Mackworth about which is thus sur-
cumscribed " Sigillum Johannis Mackworth Cleri."

Henery Mackworth ob. 3. H. 7.
=

John Mackworth who dyed in the liffe of his Father.
=

George Mackworth ob. 28. H. 8.
=

Frauncis Mackworth=Hellen 7 dau. & coheire of Humffrey
dyed. 1. Q. Elizabeth. | Hercye of Grove in Com' Nottingham.

George Mackworth.=Grace d. of Raffe Rokeby Sergeant at law.

S\[r] Thomas Mackworth of Empingham in Com' Rutland Knt. & Baronett.
=

S\[r] Henery Mack. of Empingham=Mary d. of Robert Hopton of
K\[t] and Baronett.   Wittam in Com' Somersett.

H

ADDENDA.

———◆———

CHESELDEN (see p. 21).

A Patent Graunted by Lawrence Dalton Esqr al's Norroy the last of January 1560 3 Q. Eliz. to George Cheseldine of Upinham gent. sonne of Edw. sonne of John sonne of John Cheselden late of Allaxton in Com. Leicester.

The blazon in the Patent.

Argent, a cheueron betwene 3 Crosses an crey gules; the Creast a Hound couchant Argent spotted sables, eared & collered gules, the coller garnished & fasted to the same a Lease knit together lying over his neck or.

Arms in Harl. MS. 1094.

CHESELDINE, *impaling Per pale azure and gules on three chevrons argent as many chevrons couped*   . SAYE. *Crest as in patent.*

Arms in Harl. 1558.

*Quarterly :—*1. *Argent, a chevron gules between three crosses moline gules.* (CHESELDEN.) 2. *Argent, on a fess indented sable three bezants.* (BROUGH.) 3. *Or, an eagle displayed azure, beaked and feet gules.* (MONGOMERY.) 4. SKEVINGTON.

Another Quarterly of 11 :—

1 *and* 11. CHESELDEN. 2. BROUGH. 3. MONGOMERY. 4. *Sable, three bulls' heads erased argent, a crescent gules for difference.* (SKEVINGTON.) 5. *Azure, a bend cotised between six mullets or.* (OLDLIFF.) 6. *Ermine, a bend azure.* (ENGLISH.) 7. *Sable, three garbs argent.* (CAMBRIDG, al's CLARK.) 8. *Azure, on a bend or, an annulet gules.* (DONNE.) 9. *Ermine, on a chief indented gules three escallops or.* (CHILD.) 10. *Or, a pale azure, over all a chief vert.* (COLSELL.)

———————

FLOWER (see p. 30).

"I have seene these quaterings for this Family" :—

1. *Ermines, a cinquefoil ermine.* 2. *Argent, on an escocheon azure a maunch or.* 3. *Gules, between two chevrons argent a mullet or.* 4. *Argent, on a chevron within a bordure engrailed gules three bezants.* 5. *Argent, a chevron vert between three fleurs-de-lis sable.* 6. *Azure, a cross patonce between four martlets or.* 7. *Or, a lion rampant azure, over all a bend compony or and gules.*

INDEX OF NAMES.

Martyn—*continued.*
 Richard, 17.
Massey, —, 29.
 Joane, 29.
Maude, Queen, 41.
Maudes, Cassander, 4.
 Elianor, 3.
 John, 4.
 Peter, 3.
Medowes, —, 14.
Merbury, Robertus, 22.
 Willemus, 22.
Merry, Edward, 8.
 Rose, 8.
Midleton, Anne, 23.
 Elizabeth, 8.
 John, 23.
 Sir John, 8.
Millott, *Isabell*, 1.
 John, 1.
Mollineux, Anne, 39.
 Sir John, 39.
Mongomery, 16.
Mongomery, Brigett, 22.
 Elizabeth, 22.
 Jane, 16.
 John, 16.
 Willemus, 22.
Montacute, Ellinor, 38.
 Sir Edward, 38.
Montefort, Petrus de, 22.
Montgomery, Anne, 25.
 Bridgett, 21.
 Sherrington, 25.
 William, 21.
(*Moore*), 38.
Moore, Dorothie, 25.
Morbury, William, 21.
Morgan, —, 19.
 Margarett, 19.
 Thomas, 22.
Morris, Elizabeth, 13.
 John, 13.
(*Morvill*), 38.
(*Moton*), 38.
Moton, Elizabeth, 38.
 Robert, 38.
Moulton, 7.
Mounbocher, 1, 3.
Mounbocher, Grace, 2.
 Thomas, 2.
Mountfford, Piers de, 22.
Mountffort, William, 44.
Mulsho, Mary, 20.
 William, 20.
Murdach, Henricus, 22.
(*Mutton*), 38.
Mynar, Ann, 12.
 Rafe, 12.
MYNNE, 5.
Mynne, Ann, 5.
 Catherine, 5.
 Christopher, 5.
 Elizabeth, 5.
 Frances, 5.
 Francis, 5.
 Henry, 5.
 Jane, 5.
 John, 5.
 Mary, 5.
 Nicholas, 5.
 Rebecca, 5.

Mynne—*continued.*
 Sir Henry, 5.
 Thomas, 5.
 William, 5.

(*Napton*), 45.
Naylor, James, 8.
 Jane, 8.
Neale, Anne, 43.
 Charles, 43.
 Francis, 20.
 Mary, 20.
NEDHAM, 27.
Nedham, Ambrose, 27.
 Anne, 27.
 Anthony, 27.
 Dorathey, 27, 34.
 Edward, 27.
 Frances, 27.
 Francis, 27.
 Henry, 27.
 Mary, 27.
 Richard, 27.
 Robert, 27.
 Thomas, 27, 34.
 William, 27.
Needham, —, 4.
Nevell, —, 21, 23.
 Beatrix, 23.
 Elizabeth, 21.
 Jane, 6.
 Sir Thomas, 6.
 Thomas, 22.
Neville, Stephanus de, 22.
Newers, —, 21.
Nicholls, Jane, 42.
 Robert, 42.
Noell, Andrew, 30.
 Dorothie, 30.
 Mabell, 38.
 Sir Andrew, 38.
Noone, Jane, 47.
 John, 47.
Normanville, Dwinsia de, 48.
 Galiena de, 48.
 Margarett de, 48.
 Raphe de, 48.
 Thomas de, 48.
Northumberland, Walteof,
 Earl of, 41.
Norwich, Alicia, 24.
 Simon, 24.

Obbone, Ann, 33.
 James, 33.
 John, 33.
Odine, Ann, 33.
 James, 33.
 John, 33.
Offington, Johannes de, 22.
Offley, Mary, 39.
 William, 39.
OGLE, 37.
Ogle, Jane, 7.
 Thomas, 7.
Okeover, Cassander, 12.
 Richard, 12.
Oliver, Grace, 25.
 James, 25.
Osbert, 41.
OSBORNE, 18.
Osborne, Elizabeth, 18.

Osborne—*continued.*
 George, 18.
 James, 18.
 John, 18.
 Thomas, 18.
 Winnifred, 18.
OVERTON, 16.
Overton, Alice, 16.
 Ann, 16.
 Barbara, 16.
 Bartholomew, 16.
 Dorothy, 16.
 Dymok, 16.
 Edward, 14, 16.
 George, 16.
 Jane, 16.
 Joane, 16.
 Katherin, 14, 16.
 Lucie, 16.
 Mary, 16.
 Thomas, 16.
 William, 16.
Owen, Elizabeth, 3.

Page, —, 30.
 Agnes, 30.
 Alicia, 24.
 Edmond, 30.
 Ellenor, 30.
 George, 24.
(*Pakeman*), 17.
Pakeman, Catherine,
 17.
 Simon, 17.
PALMER, 24.
PALMER, 36.
Palmer, —, 20, 48.
 Alicia, 24.
 Anna, 24.
 Edwardus, 24.
 Elizabetha, 24.
 Ellina, 24.
 Galfridus, 24.
 Georgius, 24.
 Isaabell, 25.
 Katherina, 24.
 Margarett, 24.
 Richardus, 24.
 Simon, 24.
 Thomas, 24.
 William, 24, 25.
Parker, —, 27.
Partrich, —, 17.
 Ann, 17.
Pawlen, —, 28.
Peach, Nicholas, 40.
 Richard, 40.
 Sabina, 40.
PECK, 27.
 Peck, Alice, 6.
 Anthony, 27.
 Christopher, 27.
 Dorothy, 27.
 Elizabeth, 27.
 Henry, 27.
 Honor, 27.
 John, 27.
 Luke, 27.
 Richard, 6.
 William, 27.
Peers, Isaabell, 41.
 Thomas, 41.

I

LONDON: PRINTED BY TAYLOR AND CO., LITTLE QUEEN STREET, LINCOLN'S INN FIELDS.

The Harleian Society,

INSTITUTED FOR THE

PUBLICATION OF INEDITED MANUSCRIPTS

RELATING TO

GENEALOGY, FAMILY HISTORY, AND HERALDRY.

~~~~~~~~~~~~~~~~~~

President.

HIS GRACE THE DUKE OF MANCHESTER.

Vice-Presidents.

THE RIGHT HON. VISCOUNT MIDLETON.
THE RIGHT HON. LORD MONSON.
THE HON. HENRY ROPER-CURZON.
SIR GEORGE F. DUCKETT, BART., F.S.A.
SIR HENRY VAVASOUR, BART.
SIR JOSEPH RADCLIFFE, BART.
RALPH ASSHETON, Esq., M.P.
EVELYN PHILIP SHIRLEY, Esq., F.S.A.
R. E. EGERTON-WARBURTON, Esq.

Council.

W. AMHURST TYSSEN AMHURST, Esq.
GEORGE W. MARSHALL, Esq., LL.M.
GRANVILLE LEVESON GOWER, Esq., F.S.A.
JOSEPH JACKSON HOWARD, Esq., LL.D., F.S.A., *Hon. Treasurer.*
THE REV. SAMUEL HAYMAN, M.A.
GEORGE J. ARMYTAGE, Esq., F.S.A., *Hon. Secretary.*
COLONEL JOSEPH LEMUEL CHESTER.
JOHN DAVIDSON, Esq.
JOHN MACLEAN, Esq., F.S.A.
WENTWORTH STURGEON, Esq.
JOHN FETHERSTON, Esq., F.S.A.
FAIRLESS BARBER, Esq., F.S.A.

Bankers.

LONDON AND COUNTY, 21, Lombard Street.

Auditors.

LIONEL G. ROBINSON, Esq., Junior Athenæum Club, and
Audit and Exchequer Office.
DUDLEY CARY ELWES, Esq., F.S.A., South Bersted, Bognor.

Rules.

1. This Society shall be called the HARLEIAN SOCIETY.

2. It shall have for its chief object the publication of the Heraldic Visitations of Counties, and any manuscripts relating to genealogy, family history, and heraldry, selected by the Council.

3. The Council shall consist of a President, nine Vice-Presidents, and twelve Members of Council, two of whom shall hold the posts of Secretary and Treasurer; and any four, including the Treasurer or Secretary, shall form a quorum. In case of equality of votes, the Chairman to have a casting vote. Any Candidate may be elected with the consent in writing of one Member of the Council, the Treasurer, and the Secretary.

4. Three Members of the Council shall retire in rotation annually, but shall be eligible for re-election.

5. The Annual Subscription shall be One Guinea, paid in advance, and due on the 1st day of January in each year; and Members elected after two hundred and fifty shall have joined, shall pay an Entrance Fee of 10s. 6d. in addition to their first Annual Subscription.

6. The funds raised by the Society shall be expended in publishing such works as are selected by the Council.

7. One volume at least shall be supplied to the Members every year.

8. An Annual Meeting shall be held in the month of June every year, at such time and place as the Council may direct; and due notice shall be sent to the Members of the Society at least a fortnight previously.

9. No work shall be supplied to any Member unless his Subscription for the year be paid; and any member not having paid his subscription for two years, having received notice thereof, shall cease to belong to the Society.

10. The Council may, at their discretion, pay the expense of transcribing from manuscripts whenever two hundred Members, at least, shall have joined the Society; but no payment in money shall be made to any person for editing any work for the Society.

11. No copies of the Publications of the Society shall be supplied to persons not actually Members, and each Member shall be restricted to a single Subscription.

12. An account of the receipts and expenses of the Society to be made up to the 1st of June in each year, and published with a list of the Members and the Rules of the Society in the following volume.

13. These Rules shall not be altered except at the Annual Meeting, and three clear weeks' notice must be given to the Secretary of any such intended alteration.

The Council has selected the Visitation of Oxford in 1574 and 1634 to follow that of Rutland.

Report for the Year 1869-70.

On the 27th of March, 1869, two Members of the Society's Council invited several of their friends and correspondents to assist in the formation of a Society, having for its special object the publication of the Heralds' Visitations of Counties and other important Genealogical Manuscripts. By the 28th of May, fifty-eight persons signified their willingness to co-operate in the establishment of such a Society, and at a Special Meeting held on that day at 8, Danes Inn, the Honourable HENRY ROPER-CURZON in the Chair, the Officers of the Society were appointed and the Rules drawn out. The success that the Society met with was so great, that by the 28th of July no fewer than one hundred Members had joined, and from that time to the present this number has been gradually increasing, so that now it exceeds one hundred and seventy Members.

This great success may be attributed to the exertions of the several Members of the Council, and to the literary status of many of the original Members.

The Society has already published and distributed 'The Heraldic Visitation of London, taken by Robert Cooke, Clarenceux, in 1568,' edited by JOSEPH JACKSON HOWARD, F.S.A., and GEORGE J. ARMYTAGE, F.S.A.

Camden's 'Visitation of Leicestershire in 1619,' edited by JOHN FETHERSTON, F.S.A., will be ready for circulation in about a fortnight. This is a large work, and contains 207 pages of pedigree matter only. It will also include facsimiles of several of the signatures of the heads of families who entered their pedigrees at that Visitation, together with a very elaborate armorial and general index.

Sir GEORGE F. DUCKETT, Bart., F.S.A., has offered to edit a Visitation for the Society; and the 'Visitation of Nottingham,' to be edited by G. W. MARSHALL, Esq., LL.M., is ready for the press; and the three Oxfordshire Visitations are now being prepared by Mr. WILLIAM HENRY TURNER, of Oxford.

The Society is now in a position to print Two Volumes a year, and it is hoped that the addition of another hundred Members will enable a third volume to be published; and it is believed that the issue of Three Volumes in return for the Guinea Subscription will place the Society in the foremost ranks of such Associations of this country.

The especial thanks of the Members are due to the Council of the Surrey Archæological Society for so courteously placing their Meeting-room at the disposal of the Harleian Council. Arrangements are now being made for the payment of a few pounds per annum to the Surrey Society, as it is considered desirable that this Society shall have a recognized place of meeting.

Harleian Society.

BALANCE SHEET FOR THE YEAR ENDING 31st MAY, 1870.

Dr.

		£	s.	d.	£	s.	d.
1869. 141 Subscriptions at	21s.	148	1	0			
2 "	21s. 6d.	2	3	0			
3 "	20s.	3	0	0			
					153	4	0
1870. 37 "	21s.	38	17	0			
1 "	20s.	1	0	0			
					39	17	0
					£193	1	0

Cr.

	£	s.	d.	£	s.	d.	£	s.	d.
Receipt Stamps							0	8	4
Commission on Cheque							0	0	6
Advertisements—									
'Athenæum'	£1	8	0						
'Notes and Queries'	2	1	6						
							3	9	6
Incidental Expenses—									
Honorary Secretary							5	14	1
Honorary Treasurer							1	6	6
Circulars, etc.							6	12	0
Printing and Binding London Visitation							87	0	0
							104	10	11
Balance in hand on 31st May, 1870							88	10	1
							£193	1	0

We have carefully examined the foregoing accounts, and find them correct in every particular and the payments supported by the necessary vouchers.

DUDLEY G. CARY-ELWES, } *Auditors.*
LIONEL G. ROBINSON, }

List of Members,

G. BRINDLEY ACWORTH, F.S.A., Star Hill, Rochester.
EDWARD AKROYD, M.P., F.S.A., Bank Field, Halifax.
REGINALD AMES, Cote House, Westbury-on-Trym, Bristol.
W. AMHURST T. AMHURST (*Council*), Didlington Hall, Brandon.
FRANK ANDREW, Ashton-under-Lyne.
ELY ANDREW, Mere Bank, Ashton-under-Lyne.
J. E. ANDREWS, War Office.
CHARLES FREDERICK ANGELL, F.S.A., Grove Lane, Camberwell, S.E.
WILLIAM SUMNER APPLETON, Boston, U.S.A.
FRANCIS R. ARMYTAGE, Balliol College, Oxford.
GEORGE J. ARMYTAGE, F.S.A. (*Hon. Secretary*), Kirklees Park, Brighouse.
The EARL of ARRAN, The Pavilion, Hans Place, S.W.
RALPH ASSHETON, M.P. (*Vice-President*), Downham Hall, Clitheroe.
JOHN ASTLEY, Broad Gate, Coventry.
Rev. CHARLES S. ATKINSON, Harswell, York.
W. J. ST. AUBYN, 68th Light Infantry, Fort Camden, Cork.

Lieut.-Col. BAGNALL, Shenstone Moss, near Lichfield.
CHARLES BAKER, F.S.A., 11, Sackville Street, Piccadilly, W.
Mrs. BAKER, Ulster Terrace, Regent's Park, N.W.
FAIRLESS BARBER, F.S.A. (*Council*), Castle Hill, Rastrick, near Brighouse.
JOSEPH GURNEY BARCLAY, 54, Lombard Street, E.C.
THOMAS H. BATES, Mayfield, Wolsingham.
JOHN BATTEN, F.S.A , Aldon, Yeovil.
GEORGE FREDERICK BEAUMONT, Knowle, Fixby, Huddersfield.
Rev. CHARLES W. BOASE, 33, Surrey Street, Strand, W.C.
THOMAS WILLIAM BOORD, F.S.A., 180, Belsize Road, Kilburn, N.W.
W. CONSITT BOULTER, F.S.A., 6, Park Row, Park Street, Hull.
EDMUND M. BOYLE, Rockwood, Torquay.
CHARLES HOLTE BRACEBRIDGE, The Hall, Atherstone, Warwickshire.
Lieut.-Col. BRADBURY, Huddersfield,
The Rev. WILLIAM BREE, the Rectory, Allesley, Coventry.
The Hon. and Rev. R. O. BRIDGEMAN, Weston-under-Lyziard, Shifnal.
THOMAS BROOKE, Armitage Bridge, Huddersfield.
FRANCIS CAPPER BROOKE, Ufford Place, Woodbridge.
The Rev. FREDERICK BROWN, F.S.A., Fern Bank, Beckenham, Kent.
PERCY C. S. BRUERE, Middleham, Bedale, Yorkshire.
The Rev. JOSEPH BUCKLEY, M.A., Sopworth Rectory, Chippenham.
W. E. G. LYTTON BULWER, Quebec House, East Dereham.
CHARLES JOHN BURGESS, Naval and Military Club, London, W.
SIR BERNARD BURKE, C.B., LL.D., Ulster King-of-Arms, Dublin.
JOHN BUTLER-BOWDEN, Pleasington Hall, Blackburn.

BENJAMIN BOND CABBELL, F.R.S., F.S.A., 52, Portland Place, W.
F. TEAGUE CANSICK, 28, Jeffrey Street, Kentish Town, N.W.
R. BROWN CANSICK, 2, Bedford Gardens, Kensington, W.
The Dowager Countess of CARNARVON, Pixton Park, Dulverton.
GEORGE ALFRED CARTHEW, F.S.A., East Dereham, Norfolk.
THOMAS CHAPMAN, F.R.S., F.S.A., 25, Bryanstone Square, W.
COLONEL J. L. CHESTER (*Council*), 16, Linden Villas, Blue Anchor Road, Bermondsey, S.E.
CHETHAM'S LIBRARY, Manchester (Thomas Jones, Esq., Librarian).
The Rev. RICHARD CHUTE CODRINGTON, Haygrove, Bridgewater, Somerset.
Rev. FREDERIC T. COLBY, B.D., F.S.A., Fellow of Exeter College, Oxford.

JAMES EDWIN COLE, Easthorpe Court, Wigtoft, Spalding.
F. S. BERMINGHAM PEN COLE, Freemantle, Southampton.
SYDNEY COLE, Norwood Court, Southall, Middlesex.
JAMES COLEMAN, 22, High Street, Bloomsbury, W.C.
J. KYRLE COLLINS, Wiltondale, Ross, Herefordshire.
W. H. COTTELL, 1, Manor Rise, Brixton, S.W.
J. GREGORY COTTINGHAM, Edensor, Chesterfield.
W. PRIDEAUX COURTNEY, Ecclesiastical Commission.
Mrs. JOHN WOODHEAD CROSLAND, Thornton Lodge, Huddersfield.
EDWIN PURVES ROPER-CURZON, Upper Sheen House, Mortlake, S.W.
The Hon. HENRY ROPER-CURZON (*Vice-President*), 47, Argyle Road, Kensington.
The Hon. SIDNEY C. ROPER-CURZON, Upper Sheen House, Mortlake, S.W.

R. S. LONGWORTH DAMES, M.A., 32, Upper Mount Street, Dublin.
JOHN DAVIDSON (*Council*), 14, St. George's Place, Hyde Park Corner, S.W.
ROBERT DAVIES, F.S.A., The Mount, York.
GORDON DAYMAN, St. Giles's, Oxford.
The Rev. JOHN BATHURST DEANE, M.A., F.S.A., Sion Hill, Bath.
GEORGE DIGBY WINGFIELD DIGBY, Sherborne Castle, Sherborne, Dorsetshire.
Mrs. FETHERSTON DILKE, Maxstoke Castle, Coleshill, Warwickshire.
SIR C. WENTWORTH DILKE, Bart., M.P., 76, Sloane Street, W.
ROBERT DOWMAN, 'Manchester Guardian' Office, Manchester.
HENRY HOLMAN DRAKE, LL.D., Esplanade, Fowey, Cornwall.
SIR GEORGE F. DUCKETT, Bart., F.S.A. (*Vice-President*), Fangfoss Hall, York.
GEORGE F. DUNCOMBE, 17, St. Stephen's Road, Bayswater, W.

CHARLES EDMUNDS, Bull Street, Birmingham.
ALBERT EDWARDS, Philadelphia, U.S.A.
The Rev. HENRY T. ELLACOMBE, M.A., F.S.A., Clyst St. George Rectory, Topsham, Devon.
WM. SMITH ELLIS, Hydecroft, Charlwood, Surrey.
DUDLEY CARY ELWES, F.S.A., South Bersted, Bognor.
V. CARY ELWES, Brigg, Lincolnshire.
WILLIAM ROBERT EMERIS, M.A., F.S.A., Louth, Lincolnshire.

THOMAS FALCONER, one of the Judges of the County Courts, Usk, Monmouthshire.
J. G. FANSHAWE, Board of Trade, Whitehall, S.W.
WILLIAM FENNELL, Wakefield.
JOHN FETHERSTON, jun., F.S.A. (*Council*), High Street, Warwick.
LADY FETHERSTONHAUGH, Uppark, Petersfield.
GEORGE FITZWILLIAMS, New York, U.S.A.
EDWARD FITZWILLIAMS, Philadelphia, U.S.A.
CHARLES H. FOX, M.D., The Beeches, Brislington, Bristol.

JOHN RIBTON GARSTIN, F.S.A., 21, Upper Merrion Street, Dublin.
ARTHUR EDWARD GAYER, Q.C., LL.D., Dublin.
JOSEPH GILLOW, jun., Winckley Square, Preston.
GRANVILLE LEVESON GOWER, F.S.A. (*Council*), Titsey Park, Godstone.
HENRY SYDNEY GRAZEBROOK, Stourbridge, Worcestershire.
The Rev. HENRY THOMAS GRIFFITH, B.A., Felmingham Vicarage, Norwich.
THOMAS GRISSELL, F.S.A., F.R.S.L., Norbury Park, Mickleham, Dorking.
KELYNGE GREENWAY, Warwick.
EDWARD GREAVES, M.P., Avonside, Warwick.
GORDON GYLL, Remenham House, Wraysbury, Staines.

EDWARD HAILSTONE, F.S.A., Horton Hall, Bradford, Yorkshire.
The Rev. H. F. HALL, M.A., High Legh, Knutsford, Cheshire.
LADY FRANCES VERNON-HARCOURT, The Homme, Weobly.
JOHN HARDY, M.P., Dunstall Hall, Burton-on-Trent.
WILLIAM HENRY HART, F.S.A., The White House, St. Peter's Lane, Canterbury.
WILLIAM HARVEY, Harrold Hall, Bedford.
The Rev. SAMUEL HAYMAN, M.A. (*Council*), The Rectory, Doneraile, Ireland.

LADY HEATHCOTE, Hursley Park, Winchester.
THOMAS HELSBY, 41, Princess Street, Manchester.
ROBERT HENDERSON, Bell House, Pitminster, Taunton.
SPENCER HERREPATH, 15, Upper Phillimore Gardens, W.
WILLIAM PERRY HERRICK, Beaumanor Park, Loughborough, Leicestershire.
Miss FRANCIS MARGERY HEXT, Lostwithiel, Cornwall.
JOHN HIRST, jun., Dobcross, Saddleworth.
The Rev. C. W. HOLBECH, Farnborough, Banbury.
DANIEL DEAN HOPKYNS, F.S.A., Weycliffe, St. Catherine's, near Guildford.
JOSEPH JACKSON HOWARD, LL.D., F.S.A. (Hon. Treas.), 3, Dartmouth Row,
    Blackheath, S.E.
THOMAS HUGHES, F.S.A., 1, Grove Terrace, Chester.

Rev. EDMUND JERMYN, B.A., Nettlecombe Rectory, Taunton.
JOSEPH JONES, Abberley Hall, Stourport.
W. STAVENHAGEN JONES, 2, Verulam Buildings, Gray's Inn, W.C.
EDWARD BASIL JUPP, F.S.A., Carpenters' Hall, London Wall, E.C.

The Rev. F. W. KITTERMASTER, All Saints, Coventry.
ARTHUR JOHN KNAPP, Llanforah House, Clifton, Bristol.

C. T. LANE, 3, Lombard Court, Lombard Street, E.C.
THOMAS LAYTON, F.S.A., Kew Bridge, Middlesex, W.
The Rev. F. G. LEE, D.C.L., F.S.A., 6, Lambeth Terrace, S.W.
LEICESTERSHIRE ARCHITECTURAL AND ARCHEOLOGICAL SOCIETY.
MRS. LITTLEDALE, 19, Queen's Gate Gardens, South Kensington.
BEN. LOCKWOOD, Huddersfield.
WILLIAM H. DYER LONGSTAFFE, F.S.A., Gateshead.

JOHN MACLEAN, F.S.A. (Council), Pallingswick Lodge, Hammersmith, W.
SILVANUS J. MACY, 21, West 47th Street, New York, U.S.A.
The Rev. A. R. MADDISON, Friskney, Boston, Lincolnshire.
THE DUKE OF MANCHESTER (President), 1, Great Stanhope Street, W.
GEORGE W. MARSHALL, LL.M. (Council), Wescombe House, Bicknoller, Taunton.
BERNULF DE CLEGG MATTINSON, Oldham.
WALTER C. METCALFE, Epping, Essex.
The Right Hon. VISCOUNT MIDLETON, Peper Harrow Park, Godalming.
MINNESOTA HISTORICAL SOCIETY, St. Paul, Minnesota, U.S.A.
The Rev. JOHN MIREHOUSE, Colsterworth, Grantham.
Captain R. MOLESWORTH, High Legh, Knutsford.
The Right Hon. LORD MONSON (Vice-President), Gatton Park, Reigate.
THOMAS H. MONTGOMERY, 400, Walnut Street, Philadelphia, U.S.A.
Lieut.-Col. CHARLES THOMAS JOHN MOORE, F.S.A., Frampton Hall, near Boston.
FREDERICK J. MORRELL, St. Giles, Oxford.
EDWARD MORTON, F.S.A., The Bank, Malton, Yorkshire.
GEORGE MURRAY, Hartford House, Werneth, Oldham.

C. N. NEWDEGATE, M.P., Arbury Hall, Nuneaton, Warwickshire.
Miss NEWMAN, 6, Patshull Road, Kentish Town, N.W.
Miss CHARLOTTE NEWMAN, 6, Patshull Road, Kentish Town, N.W.
JAMES NEWMAN, 235, High Holborn, W.C.
CAPTAIN W. NEWSOME, R.E., Gravesend.
JOHN GOUGH NICHOLS, F.S.A., 25, Parliament Street, S.W.

WILLIAM JOHN O'DONNAVAN, LL.D., M.R.I.A., Foxcroft House, Portarlington.
EVAN ORTNER, 3, St. James's Street, S.W.
FREDERIC OUVRY, F.S.A., 12, Queen Anne Street, Cavendish Square.

The Rev. FIELDING PALMER, Eastcliff, Chepstow.
The Rev. JOHN PAPILLON, M.A., P.S.A., Lexdon Rectory, Colchester.
The Rev. J. T. PARKINSON, D.C.L., F.S.A., Ravendale, Grimsby.
DANIEL PARSONS, Stuarts Lodge, Malvern.

D. WILLIAMS PATERSON, Newark Valley, New York, U.S.A.
EDWARD PEACOCK, F.S.A., Bottesford Manor, Brigg, Lincolnshire.
Rev. A. J. PEARMAN, Rainham Vicarage, Sittingbourne.
CHARLES GEORGE PERCEVAL, Passenham Manor, Stony Stratford.
THOMAS A. PERRY, Bitham House, Leamington.
JOSEPH PLUCKNETT, F.S.A., Manor House, Finchley, N.
LEMUEL POPE, Cambridge, Massachusetts, U.S.A.

SIR JOSEPH RADCLIFFE, Bart. (*Vice-President*), Rudding Park, Wetherby.
The Rev. CANON RAINE, York.
J. R. RAINES, Burton Pidsea, Hull.
ALEXANDER RIVINGTON, 27, Cleveland Gardens, Hyde Park, W.
The Rev. C. J. ROBINSON, M.A., Norton Canon Vicarage, Weobly.
The Rev. EDWARD ROGERS, M.A., Blachford, Ivy Bridge, Devon.
R. R. COXWELL-ROGERS, F.S.A., Dowdeswell Court, Andoversford, Gloucester.
The Rev. ROBERT ROE ROGERS, 104, Exmouth Street, Parkfield Terrace, Birken-
head.
The ROYAL LIBRARY, Windsor Castle.
Rev. DAVID ROYCE, The Vicarage, Lower Swell, Stow-on-the-Wold.
JAMES RUSBY, 34, Manor Road, Wickham Park, Lewisham, S.E.
The DUKE OF RUTLAND, K.G., Belvoir Castle, Grantham.

EVELYN PHILIP SHIRLEY, F.S.A. (*Vice-President*), Lower Eatington Park, Strat-
ford-on-Avon.
Rev. E. H. MAINWARING SLADEN, M.A., F.R.G.S., Alton Berners, Marlborough.
J. S. SMALLFIELD, 32, University Street, W.C.
CHARLES SOTHERAN, 6, Meadow Street, Moss Side, Manchester.
CHARLES STEWART, Royal Artillery, Government House, Jersey.
WENTWORTH STURGEON (*Council*), 25, Gloucester Place, Portman Square, W.
JOHN SYKES, M.D., F.S.A., Doncaster.

Miss CAROLINE C. THAYER, Boston, U.S.A.
THOMAS THOMSON, M.D., Clarence Terrace, Leamington.
T. G. TOMKINS, Great Ouseburn, York.
GEORGE D. TOMLINSON, Huddersfield.
HENRY TREHERNE, Latymer House, Brook Green, W.
Sir J. SALUSBURY TRELAWNY, Bart., M.P., Trelawne, Liskeard, Cornwall.
Sir W. C. TREVELYAN, Wallington, Newcastle-on-Tyne.
GEORGE TUCK, New Road, Windsor.
WM. HENRY TURNER, 8, Turl Street, Oxford.
The Rev. SAMUEL BLOIS TURNER, F.S.A., South Elmham, Halesworth, Suffolk.
J. R. DANIEL TYSSEN, F.S.A., 9, Lower Rock Gardens, Brighton.
PHILIP TWELLS, M.A., Chase Side House, Enfield.

SIR HENRY M. VAVASOUR, Bart. (*Vice-President*), Holton Hall, Halesworth.

EDWARD WALTHAM, Stockwell, London, S.W.
R. E. EGERTON-WARBURTON (*Vice-President*), Arley Hall, Northwich.
EDMOND CHESTER WATERS, Upton Park, Poole.
FRANK G. WATNEY, 17, Pembridge Crescent, Bayswater, W.
JOHN WATNEY, Jun., F.R.G.S., F.S.A., 16, London Street, Fenchurch Street, E.C.
Rev. JAMES WEBB, M.A., Clifton, Brighouse.
Lieut.-Colonel WESTON, Hunterstone House, West Kilbride, Ayrshire.
WILLIAM H. WHITMORE, Boston, U.S.A.
Miss WILLIAMS, Orchard Wyndham, Taunton.
FRANCIS WILLINGTON, Tamworth, Warwickshire.
Rev. EDWARD WILTON, West Lavington, Devizes.
R. H. WOOD, F.S.A., Crumpsall, Manchester.
CHARLES H. L. WOODD, F.G.S., Roslyn, Hampstead.
W. H. WRIGHT, Philadelphia, U.S.A.

PUBLICATIONS.

PRINTED BY TAYLOR AND CO., LITTLE QUEEN STREET, LINCOLN'S INN FIELDS.